"DON'T TRY AND RESIST."

"What?" asked Jenny, confused.

The Indian woman continued. "Some of them, they try to resist, and that's when it gets bad. Just give in right away and things will be easier."

"What things?"

In the flickering candlelight inside the reeking little shack, the Indian woman's eyes narrowed. "That's something you're gonna have to find out for yourself, kid."

Jenny decided to ask. "You keep talking about *she*. But there isn't anybody else here."

The Indian woman laughed harshly. "So that's what's botherin' you! Because you can't see her?"

Jenny nodded.

The Indian woman laughed again. "Believe me, if I was you, I wouldn't be in too much of a hurry to see her." She spat an even brown stream of tobacco into a tin can resting on the floor. Then her eyes turned back to Jenny. "Nope, I wouldn't be in too much of a hurry at all."

*St. Martin's Press Mass Market titles
by Daniel Ransom*

THE FORSAKEN
THE BABYSITTER

The
BABYSITTER

Daniel Ransom

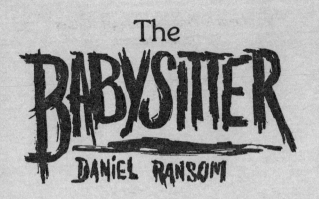

ST. MARTIN'S PRESS/NEW YORK

THE BABYSITTER

Copyright © 1989 by Daniel Ransom.

ISBN: 0-312-91583-7   Can. ISBN: 0-312-91584-5

Printed in the United States of America

First St. Martin's Press mass market edition/July 1989

10 9 8 7 6 5 4 3 2 1

From one crazed Irishman to another—
This is for Richard Laymon

1953

"DON'T PUSH HIM TOO FAST."

"No, ma'am."

"It's so dark you could hit a crack in the sidewalk and knock him right out of his wheelchair."

"Yes, ma'am."

"But don't push him too slow, either."

"No, ma'am."

" 'Cause if you go too slow, he gets bored, and then he starts swearing, and you already know too much anyway for a thirteen-year-old girl raised a good Lutheran."

"Yes, ma'am."

"And remember to respect him, 'cause he's your grandpa."

"Yes, ma'am."

"But on the other hand, don't take any guff. You know how he gets."

1

"Yes, ma'am."

"And be back by ten and no later. Don't get us all worried and having to call Uncle Bill on the police force the way we did that other time."

"No, ma'am."

And so it was on the firefly summer night of June 23, 1953, Jody left the house with her grandpa, Mr. George Emmet Tolan, a seventy-two-year-old who had suffered a stroke that left him paralyzed completely on his right side, partially on his left side, and mostly unable to speak. You could tell he could still hear, as Uncle Bob liked to say, because every time you mentioned a Republican, Gramps's eyes bulged like a drunken frog's.

Jody, new this summer to starched dresses, hair curlers, and Kotex, had a good reason to want to push Gramps tonight. This would give her the opportunity to see if a red Schwinn belonging to David Fairbain was sitting out on the sidewalk of Lorna Daily's house. David was the fourteen-year-old that Jody had a burdensome crush on, and Lorna was the most beautiful girl in the class. Down at Rexall this afternoon, sipping a lime fountain Coke, Jody had been told that David was going to pay Lorna a visit tonight. Jody wanted to see for herself if this terrible rumor was true, because once in Lorna's clutches, David Fairbain would never again be available to decent girls.

After getting home this afternoon, Jody had related all this to Mom and Uncle Bob. Not only was Lorna Daily beautiful, she'd wailed, Lorna Daily was also *short*! And with this Jody had run up the stairs to her room, with a solemn Mom and Uncle Bob following at a slower pace.

So Mom and Uncle Bob had had their first real talk

with her about boys, Uncle Bob saying at the last, "You ask me, I'd get his goat."

"His goat?" Jody asked.

"Sure. Pretend you don't care for him one whit. Nothing interests a fellow any faster than a girl who isn't interested in him." Here Uncle Bob had winked at Mom. "Or *pretends* not to be interested, anyway."

Uncle Bob and Mom had smiled at each other in a way Jody had never noticed before. Dad having been killed in Korea the year before, and Uncle Bob moving in soon after, Jody had always wondered just exactly what their relationship was. Now she was beginning to guess . . .

"So I just act not-interested?"

"Hon, you act not-interested as all get-out and then you just watch what happens."

"But Lorna's in seventh grade."

"Don't make no difference."

"And she's beautiful."

"Still don't make no difference."

"And she's *short.*"

"Short-port, who cares? You're gonna have that boy tied around your finger in two shakes of a lamb's tail." Uncle Bob always talked in "sayings" like that. Cliches, Mr. Davis her English teacher, called them.

This was about the time Jody had quit listening.

Gramps was easy to push. He couldn't eat much since the stroke and was down to about one hundred and thirty pounds. He'd never been a large man anyway, wiry and bald, with skin brown as an Indian's, a union man who still wore his UAW-CIO pin on every shirt Mom put on him.

The warm night smelled of apple blossoms and

bloomed yellow with the fat airborne bodies of fireflies. Off in the distance you could hear mothers calling their kids at the very last of the summer light, and even further off you could hear the metal roar of trains bound for the fabulous places that Dad had always promised to take her to. Dad . . .

As she pushed Gramps down the sidewalk, she could hear people on the porches, the women tinkling glasses of ice tea, the men putting church keys to cans of Grain Belt and Canadian Ace (in this factory neighborhood, the men always drank what the grocers called your "economy" brands). Luckies and Chesterfields and Pall Malls were winking their red eyes at you like bold little bugs in the gloom, and through the open window screens floated the sounds of various radio and TV shows, everything from "Boston Blackie" to newscaster Douglas Edwards talking about the coronation of Queen Elizabeth the night before, and how tired she was today.

Then, in a different and splendid neighborhood of endless lawns and homes that always intimidated Jody, they reached Lorna's house and there was no red Schwinn and Jody couldn't remember being this happy since the time Gene Autry had been at the county fair and had personally shaken her hand and called her "cutie."

No red Schwinn.

But there was something else to see, something so curious that Gramps, for the first time in months, began making sounds. Not words, he couldn't speak words, but urgent, terrified sounds. He became so agitated that she had to lean down and throw her arm around his sad frail old man's chest.

"I see it, too," she said.

Once she had seen her father and mother naked in bed

4

together and that had been pretty frightening. Another time she'd seen her collie Al car-struck and dying, his innards pink and red and blue sitting in a steaming pile on the pavement, and that had been more than frightening—horrible and unforgettable.

Yet neither scene had evoked in her what this one did. There, silhouetted on the cotton shade, she glimpsed the sight of a creature whose body was topped by a head that resembled a grasshopper's—an angular, antennaed head that moved slowly and ponderously, and seemed now to be angling toward Jody and Gramps.

Jody slapped her hands over her eyes and screamed.

Gramps surprised her by reaching and taking her hand. Feeble though he was, he wanted to comfort her. And in that moment, seeing his essential goodness, she had never loved the man so much. When she opened her eyes again, the creature had vanished from the shade, like an image from a TV screen.

After she had calmed some, she said, "God. You really think we saw it?"

Gramps, agitated, once again tried to make intelligible sounds.

Jody could sense his frustration. This was like having your tongue cut out, the way A-rabs always did in movies where Tony Curtis played guys from Bagdad and places like that.

Lorna's house, a large two-story Colonial with a gabled roof, stood alone on a corner, in the center of a furious ocean of buffalo grass.

The only way you could see directly into the front window, the way Jody and Gramps had, was to be standing where they were.

So there was no possibility of other witnesses in other houses having seen, because nobody else *could* have seen.

Just Jody, who was a kid.

And Gramps, who couldn't talk.

The only witnesses.

"You really think we saw it, Gramps?" Jody asked again, there in the sweet scent of grass newly mown and azaleas newly bloomed. "You really think we did?"

Mom always read Gramps the paper in the morning. Gramps, who had not gone through more than second grade (he couldn't remember exactly), could read but not well.

So while Uncle Bob ate his usual stack of eight pancakes (Mom was always thumping Uncle Bob on his burgeoning belly and saying, "You used to look so skinny in that white Navy uniform of yours"), Mom read Gramps bits and pieces of the paper, starting with the front page and going all the way back to the want ads.

Today's items included: Julius and Ethel Rosenberg saying they were innocent and therefore could not implicate others; an Edgar Guest ("The poet of People") poem entitled "Business Career"; a baseball player challenging Mickey Mantle's claim that he was the fastest man in the American League and daring him to race for $1000; Bela Lugosi's wife suing him for divorce on the grounds of cruelty ("Do you suppose he beat her?"); and then movie tips, one for Jody ("There's that new Martin and Lewis picture, *Scared Stiff*, starting this afternoon and you know how you love the air-conditioning in the Rialto") and one for Gramps ("Maybe tomorrow Jody could push you downtown to the RKO; they've got a new Joel Mc-Crea western picture there"); for herself Mom decided on

a Clifton Webb-Ginger Rogers movie called *Dreamboat.*
Jody wasn't sure what it was, but there was definitely
something about Clifton Webb she didn't like.

As always, Jody cleared the breakfast table, did the
dishes, and set places for lunch. All the time she did this
she was aware of Gramps, sitting feebly in his wheelchair, dressed in his faded blue workshirt now two sizes
too big for his boney frame, scribbling awkwardly on a
piece of paper with a new yellow Ticonderoga pencil.

Drying her hands, folding the nubby dishtowel neatly,
Jody turned around, sensing Gramps's faded blue gaze
on her.

He held up the piece of scratch paper he'd been drawing on with his left hand.

She recognized instantly, crude as it was, what he'd
drawn. She'd taken science all last year and so could see
the unmistakable head of a grasshopper, the two antennae thrust forward, the two lips and powerful jaws with
sharp, jagged teeth along the upper lip, and the five eyes
—the large compound eye made up of thousands of single lenses that lets the grasshopper see to the front, the
side, and to the back, and the other single eyes between
the antennae. As Mr. Solomon, the science teacher said,
"Why the grasshopper has those three single eyes is
God's secret." Gramps had added the one thing they had
not studied in science class—the reedlike tube extending
from the creature's mouth into the neck of the slumped-
over girl who had presumably been Lorna Daily. The
creature they'd seen silhouetted so briefly on the roll-up
curtain last night had had the body of a stout woman, the
head of a grasshopper, and through the reedlike tube had
either been taking something out of Lorna Daily's neck,
or putting something in.

Jody crossed the room to Gramps in two steps, snatched the paper from his hand, crumpled it up, and threw it in the wastecan along with the orange rinds and coffee grounds.

"Don't you know what they'd think if we tried to tell them what we saw, Gramps? They'd think we were crazy. Then they'd tell other people, and pretty soon everybody in Winthrop would think we were crazy."

Gramps, upset, bugged his eyes out. Jody could tell he was furious.

"I'll take you to that Joel McCrea movie today, Gramps," she said, trying to pacify him. "We won't even wait till tomorrow."

Still, he glared.

She threw herself around his useless legs, and hugged him and began to cry softly. "They'd think we were crazy, Gramps, don't you understand that? Don't you understand?"

Summer burned on. Jody saw David Fairbain at the swimming pool, at the Abbott and Costello triple feature, at the softball park, at the air-conditioned public library where Jody liked to sit and cooly read Nancy Drews, and at church.

Almost always he was in the presence of the slender, the beautifully tanned, the flashing-eyed Lorna Daily. Jody had taken Uncle Bob's advice and tried to get David's goat by virtually pretending he didn't exist. She'd walk right by him and say not a word. He always, however pointlessly, said hello and she, however reluctantly, said hello back. But he never once, according to the way Uncle Bob's plan ran, sounded sad he was with Lorna and not Jody. Not once did he sound sad.

Jody's attitude about Lorna had changed considerably. Where once she'd viewed the girl as a snake charmer, spellbinder, and devil incarnate (and all those other phrases she'd picked from Yvonne DeCarlo pirate movies), she now pitied the girl and worried about her.

The stout woman with the head of a grasshopper and the reedlike tube going into the back of Lorna's neck . . .

The first thing that made the town of Winthrop become aware of Lorna was when she stole her father's car. She took it in the middle of the night, drove it downtown, and piled right through the plate glass window of Ferguson's Department Store, knocking over the suspiciously dark mannequin that a few ladies at the Methodist church had speculated was a mulatto.

Lorna was thirteen years old the night she smashed through the window. She was also very drunk. Hendricks, the police chief who arrested her (arresting a bank president's thirteen-year-old daughter being a delicate matter), found a fifth of Wild Turkey on the seat next to her. Half of it was gone.

The next incident, two weeks later, involved the theft of a diamond ring worth five thousand dollars from Hagberg's Jewelry. Lorna took it in full view of Mr. Hagberg, and when he tried to retrieve it without incident (harmless prank, he'd been willing to say), she went berserk, scratching his face with so much fury that he required eight stitches on his right cheek. She had used only her fingernails.

The final incident, and the one from which there was no returning, involved Mrs. Hogan's black Scottie. Mrs. Hogan was what passed for old money in Winthrop, her grandfather having opened the bank where Mr. Daily was currently president. She lived two doors down from the Dailys and considered them friends.

In the middle of a terrible August afternoon ("polio weather" it was called because polio always struck when kids were forced together, because of the heat, in swimming pools and movie theaters and other public places), Mrs. Hogan heard horrible sounds from her backyard and went out to check on her Scottie.

It was there she found him dead on the lap of Lorna Daily, and it was there she found Lorna Daily feasting on the innards of the sweet little animal.

Nobody knew for sure where Lorna and her parents went. But at 6:00 A.M. next morning the wide backside of their red Packard could be seen at the City Limits sign out on the highway.

School started, the days began to grow shorter, David Fairbain took up with a transfer student from Central City who looked amazingly like Lorna Daily (though evidently the girl had no taste for live dogs), and Gramps died.

Uncle Bob found Gramps in his room. He was laid out "funeral-style" as Uncle Bob told it, hands folded over his stomach, eyes closed, obviously ready to be buried. "Just like he gave it up. Just decided it was time, poor bastard," Uncle Bob said, then backed off on the "bastard" with a scalding look from Mom. "Poor old guy," Uncle Bob amended.

Then Uncle Bob showed the sheet of notepad paper that had rested under Gramps's hands.

He waved it at both Mom and Jody. It depicted, crude as crude could be, the body of a woman with the head of a large grasshopper, a reedlike tube extending from the ragged teeth of the insect.

10

"Must've been that codeine in the cough syrup Doc Barnes gave him," Uncle Bob explained. "Makes a guy have crazy visions, like when I was on Guam and guys'd get malaria."

"May I have that?" Jody asked softly.

"Huh?"

"That piece of paper Gramps drew on," Jody said.

Uncle Bob glanced down at the paper and then at Jody. He handed it over. "Sure, hon. Sure. It's all yours."

Jody spent the rest of the day up in her room. She cried a very long time about Gramps and thought of all the neat and nice things they'd done before he'd had his stroke, and of how frail he'd been afterwards, and of how frightened she'd been for him.

Then she looked at the paper on which he'd drawn and she thought of Lorna Daily and the tube that had been placed in Lorna Daily's neck and how afterward Lorna drove the car through the plate glass window and stole the diamond ring and finally ate the little black Scottie.

Then Jody didn't cry any more.

She looked at the crude pencil drawing and did something very different.

She shuddered.

Chapter One

1

JODY HAD NEVER BEEN IN A PSYCHOLOGIST'S office before, not unless you counted that marriage counselor she'd seen at the time of her first divorce, the balding, chunky man with the big rings and the head shaved shiny like Telly Savalas, the man eager to part her legs as soon as Jody parted company with her first husband.

Or had that been her *second* divorce?

"And your relationship to Jenny, Mrs. Wagner?"

"Grandmother." She leaned over and patted the knee of her granddaughter Jenny.

The shrink, a pleasant-looking woman, seemed surprised. "But you look so young?"

Jody smiled. "I thank you for that. But I'm actually forty-nine. I have a twenty-eight-year-old daughter named Samantha, and two ex-husbands who probably don't speak very well of me." She tried to continue the smile, but by the time she got to the part about the two ex-husbands, her voice became gritty with cigarettes (though she was proud to say she smoked her last Merit eighteen months ago) and alcohol (even prouder to say that she'd had her last drink ten years ago). She smiled over at Jenny again.

They were in one of those bland modern offices, all done in dead proper earth tones and filled with new but impersonal furniture, stuff you might buy at Sears on time. The air smelled of a Mr. Coffee working very hard on a narrow stand across the room. The nicest thing about the office was the big west window through which mid-afternoon sunlight streamed, making the imitation blue-period Picasso on the wall look much better than it should have. Jody and her eight-year-old granddaughter Jenny sat on the plaid couch and Dr. Ruth Peary sat in the plaid armchair. She was a few years older than Jody and wore a simple white summer dress and beige sandals. She had exceptionally good legs and the rather short length of her dress told you that she knew it. On one arm of the chair, idly, rested a steno pad and a gold Cross pen. Dr. Peary had yet to write anything down. Jody had apparently not said anything important yet.

"Jenny lives with you?"

"No, she lives with her mother—my daughter."

"I see." With this, Dr. Peary picked up her steno pad. With one of her sandaled feet, she also depressed a button built into the side of the coffee table. Somewhere nearby, a tape recorder had just been activated. "Do you mind, Mrs. Wagner, if I ask why her mother isn't here today?"

"How about calling me Jody?"

"Fine. How about calling me Ruth?"

Jody nodded and, though she seemed about to speak,

said nothing. Instead, she placed her long, tanned, capable hands over the tiny hands of the little girl next to her. Jody had the freckles and sun-tinted long blonde hair of a teenager. Clear blue eyes, solemn and somewhat pained, glanced from the doctor to the girl. In her white blouse, denim skirt, and scuffed penny loafers, Jody managed to give the impression of being exciting and beautiful even while sitting very still. She said, "Jenny, I wonder if you'd do me a favor."

For the first time, the small red-haired girl in the very carefully ironed tan blouse and blue gauze skirt showed at least a small sign of attention. Previously, she had resembled someone in a state not unlike catatonia. Now, she angled her pretty face up to glance at her grandmother.

"Do you remember the woman at the desk in the next office?"

Jenny nodded.

"Do you remember how she asked you if you'd like a Pepsi?"

Again, Jenny nodded.

"I wonder if you'd go out there and tell her you'd like a Pepsi, and then be a very good girl and wait for me a few minutes. Would you mind?"

Jenny shook her head, her pigtails flying.

Jody bent down and kissed her. "I love you, hon. Remember that, will you?"

Two minutes later, Jenny was seated on the waiting room couch, a Donald Duck comic on her lap and a can of Pepsi in her right hand. In the doctor's office, the interview began.

"You asked why her mother wasn't here?"

"Yes."

"Her mother, who's name is Samantha and whom we all call Sam, is a cocaine addict and she's having a very bad time of it just now. I live back east. I'm a fashion illustrator. Strictly low level, so don't get any romantic notions about *Vogue* parties or anything. I do things like maternity smocks for wholesale catalogs.

"Anyway, about Sam. She's lived here in Winthrop and then moved away at least five times. Jenny came from her first marriage. We've each had two and neither of us were very good at either one of them. I moved away right after high school graduation. My mother and my Uncle Bob, whom she married when I was in eighth grade, were killed in a car accident that year. I didn't see much reason to stick around.

"I went to New York and tried a little acting and tried a little dancing and ended up doing illustrations. Sam was born in New York, but for some reason she always had a fascination for Winthrop so whenever there was an excuse—one of my class reunions or the marriage of a cousin or something—I'd bring her back here. She loves this place.

"Up until a month ago she was working as an advertising copywriter in a Chicago agency. She's divorced again —there's just her and Jenny—and the coke got to her pretty badly. She's been through three different formal programs but none of them have seemed to work. About three weeks ago, she got desperate and drove back here in the middle of the night. In the morning she rented a house from a realtor named Smythe and she and Jenny moved in. Two days ago she called me and I flew out here."

Jody paused, sighing deeply. This was one of those

times when she really wanted a cigarette. Funny, you'd think it was the alcohol she'd miss, but it was really the nicotine. Just one fresh pack of Merits . . .

"And something happened to Jenny," Jody said.

"Something?"

"You saw her. Her eyes. How pale she is. I have no idea what caused that. But she's obviously disturbed. Badly disturbed."

"Perhaps it's a reaction to her mother's problems."

Jody shook her head. "I don't think so."

"Why?"

"Because there's something Jenny won't talk about. She's started to a few times—and she has these terrible nightmares that I ask her about—but then she always stops." Jody sighed again. "That's why I brought her here. I'm hoping you can get her to talk."

Dr. Peary put down her pad. "Her mother doesn't presently have a boyfriend or anything?"

"No. Why?"

"I just wondered if we might be dealing with some kind of abuse here." She hesitated. "Does Samantha abuse her?"

Jody took it in stride. "No. She's got a very bad drug problem, but somehow she's managed to be a reasonably decent mother through it all."

"Have you taken Jenny to a GP or internist?"

"Yes. First thing after I got here."

"And?"

"And low-grade fever, a few red spots on the throat, nothing that aspirin can't handle."

"I see."

"I don't mean to insult you—Ruth—but may I ask a question?"

"Of course."

"Do you work with children very often?"

Ruth shook her head. "If you mean, am I a specialist, no. But because I'm Winthrop's one and only shrink, I do more than my share with children. So I do have a lot of practical experience."

"Good," Jody said, and there was no humor in her voice whatsoever. "Because I sense you're really going to need all of your experience. All of it."

Ruth nodded. "Why don't you go get Jenny and bring her in? Then why don't you stop back in an hour or so and pick her up? I'll make sure you and I have a few minutes to talk afterward. All right?"

"Fine," Jody said, standing up. She was still usually the tallest woman in any room. She put out her hand and shook with Ruth Peary.

Then she went to the door and asked Jenny to come in.

2

"NIKKI?"

"Yes. Hi."

"Hi. Here," he said, pushing open the Cadillac's passenger door. "Get in."

They were on a corner in downtown Winthrop, quite a busy corner actually, and more than a few people showed interest in what they were doing.

Forty-four-year-old Glen Stover had the well-deserved reputation of a chaser (his wife Marietta had filed for divorce on no less than six occasions) with a special taste for girls barely out of their teens, and certainly this one qualified—a slight, very striking brunette with a piece of cheap brown luggage in one hand and a cigarette in another. She wore a tight white T-shirt and stonewashed jeans. Beneath the T-shirt you could easily see the rose color of her precise little nipples.

Glen Stover, the local Cadillac dealer, had Hall and Oates on the tape deck, loud the way teenagers played it, and as the girl slid into the Brougham's plush leather seat, Stover found himself anxiously touching his new toupee and wondering if it was exactly in place. This one was darker than he usually wore and had a little curl in it. A secretary of his—one of those unfortunate ones who'd taken their after-hours play a little too seriously and who had to be let go, this being before sexual harassment cases started becoming so common—had told him that when he turned just a certain way and in a certain light (she'd been pretty bombed at the time), he looked not exactly but then not unlike, uh, what's-his-name, Burt Reynolds, yes, uh, Burt Reynolds.

He wondered if Nikki, in broad daylight and from the angle she was watching him, saw his resemblance to Burt Reynolds.

"How about this heat?" he said.

She nodded. "Yes. It's hot."

He liked her lips. Those little bee-stung jobs. Pouty.

"So you do this for a living, huh?"

"Right now. Till I go back to school next fall."

"You like it?"

"Very much."

"Very good," he said, laughing loud and finding his first excuse to touch her. Just a little reassuring pat on her thigh. (Nice, nice thigh; that young firm flesh; shit.) He watched her face for a reaction. Sometimes when you touched them like that, they sensed something wrong and drew away.

She just sat there. Seemingly no response one way or the other. He let his foolish heart interpret this as a good omen.

"You've had a lot of experience, I'm told."

She looked over at him. She had brown, doelike eyes, the sort that made her a woman but kept her a kid, too. She was very, very pretty. "Since I was twelve."

"Great."

"With my cousins."

"Cousins?"

"There were three of them. They lived down the block. My mother always said if you could handle them, you could handle anybody."

He laughed. "Tough ones, huh?"

"Very tough."

He couldn't raise his eyes from the persistent little nipples poking at the cotton of her T-shirt. As they sat at a stoplight across from the town library, the one with the massive stone lions on either side of the wide stairs, he anxiously touched his toupee again. He was one of those people who couldn't stand even a momentary silence, so he said, "So you're not from around here?"

"No. I graduated from high school over in Central City three weeks ago. Then I moved over here so I could be closer to the community college. I live in the brick apartment house on the corner where you picked me up. It's very nice except I have to share a bathroom."

His stomach knotted. His mother had convinced him that using other people's bathrooms was not only a filthy habit, but possibly a deadly one. All those germs. His mother, the most celebrated matron at the local country club, exerted an influence on all three of her sons, and not least on Glen. Perhaps if he hadn't had to borrow so much money from her over the years . . .

"I did mention that this is going to be a three-day job, didn't I?"

"Yes," she said, and patted the cheap suitcase on her lap.

"I mean, we'll be in town and everything, and in and out of the house, but it'll just be better if you're there all the time."

"Sure. That makes sense."

"This is the club's hundred-year anniversary. It's kind of a big deal. Hugh O'Brian's going to be there to give the keynote address and everything."

"Oh. Great."

But the way she said it, he knew she had no idea who Hugh O'Brian was. "Hugh used to play Wyatt Earp on TV back in the fifties." He smiled. "But then you wouldn't have been born till—"

"1971. April 11, 1971."

"God," he said, marveling at the thought the way others might marvel at the concept of quasars or black holes. "1971." Immediately several images filled his mind—wide ties, bell-bottomed pants, and young sumptuous chicks you just wouldn't believe. This was long before the sweat of AIDS, and right in the middle (before all those feminist bitches really started yapping) of the so-called sexual revolution. He'd worked for AT&T then as a commercial rep and he'd traveled sixteen states and, man, he'd scarcely been able to handle all the girls. (Of course, being a good father, he'd called Marietta and the kids every night, even if he didn't get to see them for weeks at a time.)

"Your children are how old?" Nikki said.

"Six and three." He sighed. Whenever he thought of the kids, he knew what a shit he was.

"That's a cute age."

"Yes, yes, it is."

"Planning to have any more?"

He felt idiotically flattered, as if she'd just complimented him on his virility. He smiled over at her and said, "No, I don't think so."

Just then the Cadillac swept up the driveway leading to a huge, Spanish-style house with a tiled roof, brilliant red against the white of the stucco and the china blue of the afternoon sky.

He heard her inhale sharply and knew that she, like most others on first seeing the family manse, was impressed. The house ran to eighteen rooms, with an eight-hole golf course in the back, a dish antenna the size of Air Force radar on the slope of the west lawn, and twenty acres of perfectly trimmed and manicured blue grass. In front of a three-stall garage sat two other Cadillacs, one a conservative blue sedan, the other a canary yellow convertible with sweeping fins that marked it as a valuable collectible.

She glanced over at him and laughed. "Is it all right if I say wow?"

For the first time, he sensed her easing up on her middle-class anxiety. "Sweetie, you can say anything you like."

"It's beautiful."

He sighed. "My brother designed it. He's an architect —a very successful one—in Chicago, and sort of the family pet. At least he's my mother's pet." Again, a note of bitterness gave his words an edge. He exhaled heavily, as

21

if unburdening himself of some intolerable truth he could no longer carry. "So you like it?"

"I've never seen anything like it." She shook her head, as if in disbelief. "My Dad's an accountant and we live in this nice little white frame house—"

This time he touched her shoulder. He had a hard time keeping his fingers away from the small tender swell of breast only inches from his grasp. He said, his voice thickening with desire, "Everything's got its price."

She shrugged. "I suppose." Then she gazed at the late afternoon shadows, a deepening blue on the perfect white walls of the house, and she said, "It just seems so peaceful here."

He thought of Marietta and all their battles over the years. There had been a time when he'd wanted Marietta just as badly as he wanted this fresh young girl here. He wondered why he'd been cursed with wanting so many women. He said, his voice still burry and his fingers still lingering on the freckled flesh of her slender shoulder, "It'll be peaceful now that you're here."

Then he did something he was instantly ashamed of because he hated guys who operated like this. Cheap-shot artists who wore pinkie rings that were always winking at you.

But he couldn't help it.

He said, "Here, let me carry that bag for you, Nikki."

And as he said this—God, just how low could he sink, anyway?—he maneuvered his hand to cross perfectly against her breast and there he felt the nub of her nipple pressing the back of his hand.

He was in an agony of joy—the moment, the beautiful moment, extended there as if in slow motion—until he

22

saw the blush start on her jawline and go all the way up her face.

She looked so young and mortified that even an aging ass-bandit like Glen Woodrow Stover had to back off and give her a break.

"Sorry," he said. Now his voice was little more than a whisper.

He went to reach for her suitcase. His fingers touched one end of it and then jumped away.

The thing was hot. Literally. Like touching a pancake griddle just as you're ready to pour on the batter.

Deftly, she swung the suitcase away from him, opened the door, and climbed out. Gone was her red face. Gone was her sense of vulnerability. There was an air of purposefulness about her now. She held the cheap suitcase tight against her leg. You could see where her tiny knuckles were white from clutching the handle so tight.

All he could think of was *hot*. What the hell could she be carrying in a suitcase that was hot like that?

"Why don't we go in and meet my wife and kids?"

"Great," she said.

As she started to walk, he saw that he could get a very nice side view of her breasts if he moved just a step or two behind her.

God, he couldn't believe it. He was walking into his own house with their weekend babysitter and he was as horned up as he used to get at fraternity parties.

By accident, he brushed the suitcase with his knee. Once more, he pulled back from the luggage, a sensation of heat searing through his body.

What the hell did she have in that thing anyway?

But then he didn't have time to think about the suitcase or her breasts or his toupee or anything at all, because his wife Marietta had opened the door and was sweetly greeting Nikki and introducing her to their two young daughters.

Inside, the first thing Nikki asked was if she could be shown to her room so she could freshen up.

As he watched her, however, Glen Stover got the idea that she wanted to unload the suitcase before anybody got a chance to look at it too closely.

While he went to the dry bar and fixed himself a dry martini, Marietta took Nikki upstairs.

Glen, feeling the gin and vermouth almost immediately, glanced down at the hand that had brushed Nikki's breast. Now he had put the mysterious suitcase out of his mind and was back on more familiar ground.

Over the years, Glen had managed to sleep with at least half a dozen of their young babysitters (that's why he was so insistent that Marietta hire only those eighteen or over, so there could be no legal repercussions).

He had this feeling, this plain lucky feeling, that Nikki was somehow going to come through for him, too.

Over his second martini, he began to make his plans more specific. Tomorrow afternoon, while Marietta was at the club helping his mother with the Founder's Day ceremony and the girls were taking their afternoon nap, he could sneak back here and . . .

He had forgotten utterly about the suitcase.

3

SO TIME TRAVEL WAS POSSIBLE, AFTER ALL, Jody thought, standing on the corner of Parsons and Main.

Merely by strolling by three blocks of dusty buildings —whose architecture ran to ornate cornices and ersatz Grecian columns and art deco lobbies left over from the thirties—Jody could recall vividly what it had been like to be a girl on these streets.

To have a Cherry Coke or lime phosphate over at the Rexall drugstore (now torn down and replaced by a red brick office building), or to see a Francis the Talking Mule movie at the State (now torn down and replaced by a concrete block building that said POLICE over its front doors), or to sit in Gibbon's Square (still thankfully intact), an ocean of green grass upon which floated a bandstand that used to be eye-hurtingly colorful on the Fourth of July with red, white, and blue bunting, or to simply sit on one of the park benches with a Cherry Ames or a Nancy Drew or a Hardy Boys if there was nothing else (she'd always secretly felt that Frank, the erstwhile hero, was largely a dork), or to go further up the street to Lyman's Union Tap and see if Uncle Bob would invite her inside, where, among the headiness of older men and their secret conversations and the smell of malt and hops and Chesterfield smoke, she'd play bumper pool and listen to Frankie Laine and Teresa Brewer records on the big Wurlitzer jukebox.

So many memories . . .

But much of it, much of downtown Winthrop—the bastards—had changed.

She stood in the waning sunlight of the day, recalling

the blaring bugles and thumping drums of holiday parades that used to march right down this very street, and how goofy yet magnificent the bandleader with his plumes and his high-stepping bravado used to look. A lurid McDonalds stood where she could see Mom and Uncle Bob and Gramps and herself (usually kneeling next to Gramps's wheelchair) eating plump mustardy hotdogs and drinking strawberry pop.

So many memories . . .

In her recollection the sunlight itself was richer, its dust motes the quick colors of fool's gold, as before her eyes passed an aqua and white 1955 Chevrolet (how thrilled she'd been the first time she'd seen one of those). And on that corner over there waved Daryl Simmons, the somewhat awkward farm kid who'd taken her to the junior prom, and who had soon after died in some place nobody had heard about, Vietnam. She saw boys with ducktails trying hard to be James Dean, and girls with pink lipstick trying hard to be Sandra Dee, and adults who looked like adults (none of this trying-to-dress-like-young-people jazz) with short haircuts and trousers worn high and dresses worn low and the air ripe with Evening of Paris and Old Spice and—

—and so many memories.

The worst of it was, she started crying.

Right there on the corner where Pearson's Bookstore used to be (where she bought *Peyton Place* for fifty cents in a plump black paperback edition and rushed home to find that it was not only sexy but good, actually a true and honest book that long remained in her memory)—

Right there with shiny new 1989 cars passing by and kids with vaguely punk hairstyles passing by and boys

with earrings passing by and girls with I'M EASY
T-shirts passing by—

She had walked the blocks that were familiar to her
and was now in the new part of downtown Winthrop.
One building was twelve stories high. There was a closed
mall with a parking lot as vast as the whole of old downtown Winthrop. There was a cop on a corner with a very
big gun and menacing mirror sunglasses (in the old days
only one cop had patrolled downtown, Gus Fenton,
plump, white-haired, and willing at any moment to sit
with you at the soda fountain in Rexall and talk about
Rocky Lane pictures—which he liked just as much as
you). And there was a four-story monstrosity that could
only be a parking garage, where way down low you actually could see big-city graffiti.

So many memories . . .

She put on her dark brown sunglasses so nobody could
see that she was crying. On her return trips to Winthrop
over the years, she'd seen the gradual changes, but none
of them had ever hit her quite this way before.

Her granddaughter Jenny's peculiar condition, no
doubt, had unnerved her.

She walked along the river now, the banks newly land-
scaped. Couples in bright summer clothes sat on green
benches beside the blue water. There was a fishy breeze
from the river and the scent of roses from the city garden
nearby. An old man with a liver-spotted face nodded
hello to her and chewed on the end of a wonderfully
malodorous cigar, and she wondered if buried inside his
fading eyes the corridors of his mind rang with the same
recollections hers did—

Then she was at a Dairy Queen. She bought herself a
Buster Bar and sat at a wobbly picnic table while next to

27

her two small brats misbehaved, their parents seemingly unable to stop them.

Then she thought of how hypocritical she was being. Jody Wagner was hardly a paragon of parenting. Hardly. Not with two husbands (both having left her because she had been unable to wean herself from the bottle) and a daughter who was a cocaine addict and a granddaughter who was presently—

She thought of Jenny's dead gaze and shivered.

What had happened to Jenny, anyway? What *could* have happened in the past few days that would so have traumatized her?

From her bout with the bottle, she'd come to understand that walking had a special calming effect on her.

She walked . . .

Up past Winthrop High with green sloping hills as a backdrop and steep, dramatic stairs in the front. A two-story red brick building, it seemed to shamble on forever. Over on the side was a cinder track surrounding a grassy field where they used to practice for cheerleading in the waning hours of hot September afternoons . . .

She walked . . .

Up past the working-class neighborhood, once fiercely proud in the way the homes had been kept, but now a jumble of littered lawns and rusty screen doors hanging by single hinges and cracked windows taped up like wounds and dead cars, stripped as if by vultures, lying ugly on front lawns long gone unmowed. There was— and God how she hated the snobbery of this term—an underclass now. In her day it had been the overriding dream of blue-collar parents to send their children to college. Looking at this bomb site of a neighborhood (the very same once neat neighborhood in which she'd grown up), she wondered what the dreams of these parents were. If they had any dreams . . .

She walked . . .

Only now she headed back toward town, the slight gold Bulova on her wrist saying it was nearly time to reclaim Jenny and see what the pleasant Dr. Ruth Peary had to say. (Why didn't Jody ever accept very pleasant people at face value? Maybe they were just as happy and well adjusted as they seemed.)

She was downtown when what appeared to be rush hour started. Bumper-to-bumper traffic came spilling out of parking lots and the lone parking garage. Horns blasted each other angrily. A cop, hot, exasperated, stood directing traffic at a light that was apparently not working. City buses, the sleek new silver kind that had been imported from Sweden, leaked black fumes into the air. The people aboard looked very happy they weren't in one of the cars.

And someone was shouting . . .

Or she thought someone was. Or she imagined someone was. With all the noise, it was hard to tell.

So she found her way back to Parsons Street and finished the short walk to the building where Dr. Peary worked. Already, she felt tension working into her shoulders and up her neck and into the lower brain.

Migraine? God, she hoped not. Sam was really out of commission and given Jenny's condition, Jody really had to be a *parent*. She had to do what so many people who had been lousy parents to their own children did—become textbook parents to their grandchildren.

She was one step from the exterior door of Dr. Peary's office when, above the honking and rumbling of buses and screeching of rubber tires on the hot pavement, she thought again she'd heard someone calling after her.

Calling her name, actually.

She started to turn and he was there, out of breath and right behind her.

He wasn't at all what she'd have expected him to become (he'd been unable to attend their two class reunions so she hadn't seen him since senior year).

For one thing, he'd put on twenty pounds. For another, his hair was almost completely gray. And for still another, properly dressed boy that he'd always been, he wore stonewashed jeans, a white button-down shirt, and a pair of black horn-rimmed bifocals that said he had some serious vision problems.

She thought back quickly: the last time she'd seen him he'd been in a blue three-piece suit and every girl who had the chance found some excuse to give him a graduation night kiss. As always in those days he'd looked mortified at PDA (Public Display of Affection), as if he'd rather be flung from a mountaintop than be treated this way in front of the other boys who'd never quite found him manly enough (not that he was wimpy exactly, just a little daydreamy).

Now he startled her completely by sliding an easy arm around her shoulder and bringing her gracefully to him so he could put a tiny tender little kiss right in the center of her forehead. At that precise moment she realized two things: how proper, in fact, he still was, and how she still felt some weird kind of kinship with him, maybe because in their class they'd both been insiders who were also, in some important secret ways, outsiders as well.

He laughed then and it was an older man's laugh, chesty and even a bit beery. "I sure as hell hope you remember who I am. I mean, you're probably not used to being accosted on the street by old guys with white hair." Then he touched her hair gently, letting it spill through his fingers like golden water. "I don't believe it. It's natural."

"Seems to be," she said, softly. She was a little bit stunned and a little bit inhibited and a little bit gaga over the last minute or so here on the street, but finally she found her voice and spoke to the man who'd long ago in that time of *Creature from The Black Lagoon* movies chosen Lorna Daily over her.

She touched his hand and half kind of patted it and half kind of shook it and said, "David Fairbain. I can't believe it. I really can't. I thought you were living in LA."

Then she smiled and thought to herself: So time travel really is possible, after all.

4

"NIGHT."
  "Dark."
  "Mother."
  "Uh, love."
  "Sweet."
  "Uh, cookies."
  "Sky."
  "Blue."
  "Sky."
  "Uh, clouds."

Dr. Ruth Peary said, "Very good. You're very quick, aren't you, Jenny. I'll bet you do well in spelldowns."

Eight-year-old Jenny shrugged inside the folds of her proper little blue dress. "Pretty good, I guess. I beat Teresa a few times."

"Teresa?"

"She was my best friend in Chicago."

"Did you like Chicago?"

For a few minutes during her session, Jenny had shown signs of emerging from her state of disorientation. It was like coming out from behind a gauzy screen. Her blue eyes had focused. Her voice had become rich with interest. She'd even wiped some dust from the toes of her black patent leather shoes.

The word association had done it. Children liked it especially. It was like a game and it allowed them to forget where they were. If you played it long enough, the children not only loosened up, they began to be honest with you, to admit some of the things that had brought them here.

Dr. Peary handed Jenny a fresh steno pad and a pencil. "Now we're going to try something new."

"Something new?"

"Yes."

"What?"

"I'm going to ask you to draw things for me."

"Draw?"

"Do you draw in school?"

"Sometimes."

"Do you like to draw?"

"Well, yes, I guess."

"Good. Then we'll draw."

"Draw what?"

"I'm going to say a word to you—just the way I did with word association—then I'd like you to draw whatever comes into your mind."

Pretty Jenny sighed and touched her toes together. "I'm not a very good drawer."

"That's all right. You don't have to be for this game."

"Okay."

Actually, Dr. Peary wasn't sure how this would go at all. Last summer she'd attended a convention in San Diego in which a Swiss shrink had projected the drawings of children between seven and ten. The shrink had pointed out that many times children would draw what they would not say.

Of course, that same convention in San Diego was where she'd met Bruce, her long-distance lover and a man who was a past master at being noncommittal. She sure hoped that this technique proved more reliable than Bruce had.

"Are you ready?"

Jenny, the steno pad open and on her lap, prepared to draw by sticking the Ticonderoga pencil in her hand. She nodded.

"All right. Let's start with the word happy."

"Happy?"

"Yes. Draw something that makes you happy."

Jenny's blue eyes gazed off distantly. For a moment, Ruth Peary feared the girl was sliding back into her state of withdrawal.

But then she bent over the pad and energetically began scribbling. When she finished, a minute or so later, she looked up.

"Good," Ruth Peary said. "Let's go on to the next word." She paused. "Sad."

"What makes me sad?"

"Yes, Jenny. What makes you sad."

Again, the thoughtful look out the window. This time was different, however. Tears welled in Jenny's eyes. Slowly, almost hesitantly, she leaned over the pad. This time she drew very carefully. The drawing completed, she gazed up at Ruth Peary with shiny, tear-filled eyes.

A lump gathered in Ruth Peary's throat. She was such a dear little girl, Jenny was; the daughter Ruth had never taken the time to have. And with Bruce foot-dragging the way he was . . .

"How about one more word?" she said, handing over a box of Kleenex Boutique tissues to Jenny.

Jenny deftly plucked one from the box and put it to her nose.

She very properly set the used Kleenex in the big orange ceramic ashtray (Some of Ruth Peary's patients still liked to smoke).

"Before I give you the last word, I'd like to ask you a question."

Apprehension showed in Jenny's eyes.

"But I want you to understand something."

"What?"

"You don't have to answer."

"I don't?"

"No, if it's something you'd rather keep to yourself, I'll understand."

"You will?"

"Yes."

"And you won't be mad?"

"I won't be mad in the least."

"You promise?"

"I promise."

Jenny said, "I guess it's okay if you ask then."

Ruth Peary paused a moment and said, "Your grandmother seems to feel that something happened to you in the last few days."

Ruth Peary was astounded by the pall that came over the eight-year-old's face. Fear? Horror? Terror? Her expression contained each of these, but there was more, too. Her body language was remarkable. She drew her arms and legs together very tightly and seemed to crawl backwards up the couch; she looked as if she wished she could continue right on up the wall till she reached the ceiling and had at last escaped Ruth Peary's office.

"Are you all right, Jenny?"

"I'm not supposed to talk about it."

"Pardon me?"

"I'm not supposed to talk about it."

"Talk about what?"

Jenny put her head down. "The other night."

Ruth Peary had encountered this tactic before, albeit not accompanied by this kind of—apprehension.

Jenny did not want to talk.

Ruth Peary said, softly, "Jenny, do you remember what I said?"

Head still down.

"I said that you didn't have to answer if you didn't want to."

Head still down.

"And I'm as good as my word, Jenny. You don't have to talk about it at all." Beat. "Are you listening, Jenny?"

When Jenny raised her head, something different—something new and startling—was in her eyes, but Ruth Peary could not decide exactly what.

Suddenly it struck her.

The high cheekbones and soft mouth, so feminine before, had suddenly assumed a tight, feral look. Jenny was no longer pretty at all.

Spittle shone on the left edge of her mouth and began running down her chin.

For a reason she did not understand, Ruth Peary became abruptly afraid of this little girl. She glanced down at her own arm and felt goose bumps. Acid had begun working its painful way up from her stomach. Here she was, an adult, sitting in an office in broad daylight with a little girl—and she was afraid?

"Jenny," she said.

"What?"

That was the most startling change of all, the deepening and coarsening of her eight-year-old voice.

"Why don't we draw now."

"Draw?"

"Yes. On your pad. With the pencil."

Ruth Peary had the eeriest sensation that she was no longer talking to Jenny, but rather to a stranger inhabiting Jenny's body. One who didn't understand what drawing meant.

"Are you ready?"

Spittle came out of the other side of Jenny's mouth. She looked like a rabid dog.

Jenny raised her pencil. Her eyes, streaked red now, glared at the doctor.

"Fear. That's the word. Fear, Jenny."

A low rumbling started in Jenny's chest and spread up through her throat and out her mouth. Ruth Peary had never heard a human being make a sound like that before.

Surprisingly, Jenny drew quickly, unhesitatingly. Then she stopped and for a moment all the new qualities of her face—the strange eyes, the foaming mouth, the angular cheeks—were masked again by Jenny's real face.

The eight-year-old was beginning to cry. "I'm not supposed to tell anybody," Jenny said. "Not anybody."

Now she sounded as frightened as Ruth Peary herself had been a little bit ago.

"What aren't you supposed to tell me?"

The low, rumbling sound came up from Jenny's chest again. Suddenly the little girl, her mouth once more running with spittle, her eyes crazed now, jumped up from the couch and flung the steno pad in the doctor's face.

The metal spirals of the pad caught Ruth Peary across the mouth. The pad had been flung so hard that the impact was painful enough to draw blood from the doctor's lip.

The pad falling to her lap, Ruth Peary looked at the page Jenny had last drawn on.

She couldn't believe what she saw there.

The sketch had been rendered with real skill, enough so that when Ruth Peary saw what the sketch depicted, she shuddered as she had shuddered few times in her life.

Sketched on the pad was the body of a girl—only in place of a human head was the head of a grasshopper with a tube of some kind sticking from its mouth.

The doctor looked up just in time to see that Jenny had raised one of the patient chairs over her head and was throwing it through the window.

37

The sound of shattering glass was incredibly loud and amazing on the soft summer air.

Then Jenny spun around and faced Ruth Peary.

Ruth Peary, unable to help herself any longer, screamed as the little girl lunged at her like an attacking animal.

Chapter Two

1

ON THE LATE AFTERNOON AIR, THE SCREAMS from the second floor had the impact of gunshots.

Jody, whose hand had been resting on the handle, now threw the door back and proceeded to pound up the steps two at a time, vaguely aware that David Fairbain was following her.

The screams continued, joined now by smashing sounds, as if burglars were trashing offices on the second floor.

Somehow, Jody knew with terrible certainty that the sounds could only be coming from Dr. Peary's office. But she couldn't guess as to what was going on.

Hot and breathless by the time she reached Dr. Peary's door, Jody leaned her weight into turning the knob and flung the door inwards.

The reception area with its desk, couch, and Chagall prints was empty.

The furious sounds of battle and occasional screams came from the interior office. By now—and surprisingly —she had realized that the person screaming was not Jenny but Dr. Peary.

David Fairbain beat her to the second door. He flung it open, and just had time to duck as a heavy ceramic coffee mug came flying out of the doorway, narrowly missing his head, and smashing into three large, jagged pieces against the jamb.

At this close range, Dr. Peary's screams were shrill. Jody, following them like a beacon, hurried into the interior office.

The place was a ruin of smashed and overturned furniture, wallpaper stained with ink, coffee, and blood, and a large window shattered into a crystal cobweb.

In the center of the office stood Jenny. At first Jody did not recognize her. Her face was angular, her eyes somehow not the same color, and the low, guttural sounds she made unimaginable coming from an eight-year-old girl.

Behind the overturned couch, Jody found Dr. Peary. The woman looked dazed. Blood streamed down the left side of her head from a good-sized wound above her temple. She alternated sobbing with shrieking.

Near her, laid out as if ready for her coffin, was Dr. Peary's nurse. Apparently, like the psychologist, the receptionist had been struck in the head. In the receptionist's case, the blow had been enough to render her unconscious.

David Fairbain went over to the nurse, crawling behind the overturned couch so he would not be hit by the cups and drinking glasses Jenny was furiously dispatching—and reached the nurse. The first thing he did was lift her wrist and check her pulse. He nodded okay to Jody.

Fairbain next went to Dr. Peary and took her in his arms, cradling her as he would a child.

It was left to Jody to stop Jenny.

She proceeded deeper into the office, ducking left and right as the child continued to hurl objects as various as paperweights and telephones.

She had an inappropriately funny thought as she moved closer and closer to her granddaughter: how she must have looked like Superman dodging bullets, the way he used to on the TV show of the fifties.

But there was nothing funny here. Nothing.

"Jenny," she said.

But she had the distinct impression that she was not talking to the Jenny she knew. The Jenny she knew did not have bulging, red-streaked eyes and silver-spittle lips; nor was the Jenny she knew psychotically destructive.

Jenny hit her with the corner of a Rolodex she threw. It sailed past with its white cards flying from the center like feathers off a hunting bird that had just been shot.

The blow was sufficient to stun Jody, but not enough to knock her down or draw blood.

"Jenny," she said again.

Her answer this time was the low, animal growl she'd heard before.

Turning slightly, following Jenny's gaze, she saw David Fairbain coming up from behind her. "We'll both grab her," Fairbain whispered.

But just as he said that, Jenny threw, with great force and precision, a tape recorder the size of a phone book right at David Fairbain's face.

The impact was enough to knock him over backwards,

his arms flailing wildly, blood already streaming from his forehead.

Jody knew she didn't have any choice now. Her plan had been to soothe and calm Jenny. That would never work. She had no idea what was going on here, but soothing and calming were not going to stop it, whatever it was.

She dove for Jenny, virtually tackling her, slamming the youngster to the floor, and then putting her weight on top of her so she couldn't move.

"Jenny! Jenny!" Jody shouted. "Don't you know who I am? I'm your grandmother!"

Once more, the grumbling sound came from within the child's chest.

At the sound, Jody felt goose bumps cover her body as if she were in ice.

Jenny's fingers were like talons on Jody's cheek. She drew a tiny line of blood at once and tried to dig more deeply but Jody jerked her head away.

David Fairbain, appearing as if from nowhere, knelt next to the girl now and pinioned her arms on either side of her head. Jenny cursed and lashed her legs out at the air, trying to get out from under their grasp. Her eyes had clouded over to a milky blue color, one that Jody could not bear to see.

Almost at once, and for no reason that Jody could understand, Jenny stopped.

Like that.

For a horrible moment, Jody had the impression that perhaps the eight-year-old had suffered a fatal heart attack.

Quickly, Jody put her head to Jenny's chest. The heartbeat was there, but faint.

"Do you know a doctor to call?" she said to David Fairbain. She was half-aware that she was shrieking.

David got up and tried to put the phone back together. Jenny had torn it into several parts.

"I'll have to go down the hall," David said, and disappeared.

Jody stayed there with Jenny. Behind the couch, Dr. Peary and her assistant were moaning and getting to their feet.

2

AN HOUR LATER, A DOCTOR NAMED FRED Cummins finished examining Jenny. He gave her a sedative that put her quickly to sleep. David Fairbain lifted the girl in his arms and then took her down to the car, where he laid her gently on the back seat of Jody's Buick station wagon.

Jody stayed in the shambles of the office, talking with Ruth Peary, who looked as if she were in need of a sedative herself.

Jody felt embarrassed for all of them—herself included—but even more she felt a desperate need to understand what could have caused her granddaughter to behave this way.

Dr. Cummins, a paunchy man in a tan summer-weight suit grown too small for him, stood with the two women as Ruth Peary recounted her session with Jenny.

"She started making these—sounds," Ruth Peary said, obviously still shaken by it all.

They stood in the receptionist's office. There was no place to sit. All the furniture had been destroyed.

"In her chest?" Jody asked, recalling the peculiar noises Jenny had made as Jody had tried to approach her.

Ruth Peary nodded.

Dr. Cummins, who constantly adjusted his eyeglasses, said, "What brought on the violence?"

Ruth Peary shrugged. "I just asked her what was troubling her."

"And she didn't say?" Dr. Cummins asked.

"Not really. Just that something happened the other night." Now the psychologist looked at Jody. "Has she said anything at all to you? Given any hint?"

Jody shook her head. "No. Nothing." She felt hollowed out. A certain deadness came over her as she looked once more around the two offices and the destruction an eight-year-old girl had visited on them. Could Jenny really have done this? Her own little granddaughter?

Dr. Cummins said, "I'd at least give some consideration to putting her in the hospital temporarily. St. Ignatius has a very good third floor."

Jody turned back to the doctor, understanding and half-resenting the unspoken implication of his words. "Third floor," of course, was code for mental hospital. Many hospitals had them but somehow they were never called that. Instead they were referred to as "special wings" or "third floors." Jody was familiar with the parlance because of all she'd gone through with her daughter Sam over the past few years. Cocaine addicts often ended up on the third floor.

Jody said, "What do you think about that, Ruth?"

Ruth Peary sighed. "To be honest, Jody, I'm afraid of

what's going to happen when she comes out of the sedative. She's very disturbed. Much more so than I thought initially."

To Dr. Cummins, Jody said, "Can you give me some kind of oral sedatives?"

Dr. Cummins touched a pudgy hand to his gray, carefully sprayed hair. "I suppose I could. If you feel adequate to—"

"She's my granddaughter."

Dr. Cummins grimaced. "You're getting defensive here, and there's no need to. We're just trying to help Jenny."

"I'm not sure that putting her in a hospital is the first solution we should try," Jody said. "I assume she'd feel a lot better waking up in familiar surroundings than in a strange room with nurses all over the place."

Ruth Peary patted Jody's hand gently. "I think she's right, Dr. Cummins. Maybe we should try to keep her at home if at all possible. Jody can bring her back in a day or so, and we can try to talk again. Sedatives should help us work through our session without—" She glanced around the room. It was a depressing sight.

Dr. Cummins went over to an end table and righted it. "What if she gets destructive again?" he asked Jody. "Are you going to be able to handle it?"

"I think so," Jody said. But obviously there was some hesitancy in her voice.

Dr. Cummins remained skeptical. "I can see you love your granddaughter, but shouldn't you be consulting her mother on this decision?"

"Her mother is—indisposed," Jody said.

Dr. Cummins glanced at Ruth Peary. "I see." Then,

"Do you still think it's worth a chance, Dr. Peary—sending Jenny home, I mean?"

"Yes."

Dr. Cummins, who obviously did not agree, sighed. "I'll write you a prescription for two different kinds of medicine. If anything should keep her calm, these should. But you'll have to watch for side effects—rashes on her arms or sores in her mouth. If either of these develop, let me know, and we'll try something else." Dr. Cummins's manner was growing more cordial now that the final decision had been made.

"Thank you, Doctor."

"Also, if you wouldn't mind, I'd like to speak with Dr. Peary alone for a moment."

"Of course." Jody looked into the inner office. "I'll just go in there and start trying to pick things up."

Dr. Cummins nodded.

Five minutes later, when Jody had finished putting all the furniture back on its legs and had picked up much of the broken glass and smashed office items, she saw that only the smaller things had been broken. The furniture was mostly intact. The check she would have to write Ruth Peary would not be as much as she'd first feared. Jody did not exactly have cash to burn.

She was just putting a chair back in place when the spiral notebook fell from inside the overturned chair to the floor.

A cold jolt of recognition rocked Jody as she gazed down at the unmistakable pencil drawing on the page the notepad was turned to.

Almost reluctantly, she knelt down and picked the pad up, flipping through the pages at once. There were other

46

drawings, but none of any particular interest. She flipped back to the last page.

Just then Ruth Peary came into the office.

"Well," she said, smiling. "This doesn't look bad at all. Thanks so much, Jody."

Jody nodded. "I'd appreciate it if you'd add up the damages and let me know what I should make the check out for."

Ruth Peary leaned in and gave her a small hug. "I'm sorry this is all coming down on your shoulders."

Jody, clear-eyed, her voice almost without emotion, said, "Penance."

"Penance?"

Jody sighed. "I wasn't a very good mother—just as Sam's real father and stepfather weren't very good fathers. Between the three of us we managed to raise a very beautiful but very insecure young woman who as yet hasn't been able to cope with the fact that she's now a mother herself." Another sigh. "So it's now my duty—my penance, if you will—to step in and take over with both my daughter and granddaughter." She laughed. "It took me forty-two years to grow up. It's about time, don't you think?" She pointed to the couch on which Ruth Peary's patients sat. "I probably should come and see you myself."

"You know something?"

"What?"

"I'd like that." Ruth Peary held up a halting hand. "And I don't mean professionally, either, though we might get around to discussing your past sometime, I suppose." She tried a small smile that was devoid of humor. "The fact is, I'm in need of a friend myself at the moment. I'm trying to get out of a relationship with one of those men who just can't make a commitment and—"

Jody said, "Believe me, I've been there, Ruth. My second husband was like that particularly. He had a mistress and he kept going back and forth between us. He just couldn't decide which of us he liked better—the nubile young coed or his rapidly aging wife."

"But you're beautiful," Ruth Peary protested.

"Perhaps. But I was also over forty and had little laugh lines around my mouth and eyes, and all that seemed to bother my husband a great deal. He was just one of those men whose ego needed constant reinforcement." She smiled. "A lot of times when we'd take Sam out—when she was in her late teens, I mean—he'd always walk closer to her, so people would think she was his woman and not me."

"That's pretty sad."

Jody smiled and not without bitterness. "If you knew Ken, you'd also know it was pretty funny. He was twenty pounds overweight and completely bald."

"But in his mind," Ruth Peary said, "he was Robert Redford."

"Exactly." Then her eyes fell to the notepad and she said, "I'd like to ask you where this came from."

"Jenny drew it."

"I was afraid you'd say that."

"Sometimes I have patients draw out their word association subjects. I said the word fear to Jenny and this was what she drew."

"Did she say anything else about it?"

"No." Ruth Peary thought a moment. "She had just finished saying that she wasn't supposed to talk about what had happened the other night. Then she drew this and—" Ruth Peary shook her head, obviously remembering Jenny's sudden and terrifying violence. "Then she got up and lunged at me. I got behind the desk. I felt very foolish for a second. I'm supposed to be the adult and in charge of all the situations in this office—yet there I was hiding from an eight-year-old girl."

"I would have been hiding, too, believe me."

Ruth Peary touched the notepad. "Do you know what that represents?"

The page she referred to depicted the woman with the head of a grasshopper.

"I'm afraid I do, yes. But I can't quite believe it." She paused. "And I'd like to talk to Jenny some more before I go into any more detail. If you don't mind."

Ruth Peary seemed vaguely disappointed, but she put on her best professional face and said, "No, that's fine. Whenever you're ready to talk, so am I."

Jody looked up from the pad. "Do you have any clinical sense of what's going on with Jenny?"

"I wish I had."

"Can you make any guess as to how she'll act when she comes out of the sedative?"

"If you keep her on the medication Dr. Cummins prescribed, I don't think you'll have too much trouble. The dosage of Xanax he gave her, for instance, will keep her asleep much of the time."

Jody's eyes fell to the pad again. As she looked at the hideous drawing and felt all the memories it evoked in her, she said, "Have you ever seen any other young patient behave this way in Winthrop before?"

"Why are you limiting it to Winthrop?"

Jody tapped the notebook and sighed. "I know what this drawing represents."

"You do?"

"Yes." She hesitated. "When I was thirteen, I—" Then she stopped herself. She had never been able to discuss with anybody but Gramps what they had seen silhouetted that night on Lorna Daily's shade-drawn window.

"Yes?"

"Well," Jody said, "let's just say I know what this is."

"And you want to know if I've ever seen this kind of behavior before in Winthrop?"

"Right."

"No. But the strange thing is, I've heard about it."

"You have?"

"Yes. Dr. Malbourne, the man I succeeded in this office, he told me of three or four cases of local children who had just suddenly gone berserk, gotten really violent and—" Now it was Dr. Peary's turn to hesitate and become evasive.

Quietly, almost as if she didn't want to hear the answer, Jody said, "And what happened to those children?"

Ruth Peary touched Jody's hand again. "It doesn't mean it will happen to Jenny."

"Please," Jody said. "What happened to the children?"

"They had complete breakdowns and had to be permanently institutionalized."

Jody thought of Lorna Daily. She wondered what had happened to the girl after her family had so abruptly left Winthrop following the incidents with the car and the dog.

Then Jody's eyes lifted and looked out the window at her Buick station wagon in the parking lot.

Institutionalized.

Permanently.

Helplessly, tears formed in the corners of Jody's eyes and she said, "Thank you, Ruth. I'll be in touch soon."

Then she was gone down the stairs, two at a time, needing to stand in the air, in the warmth of the day and the noise of the traffic and the exhaust of buses—somehow they all seemed reassuring, given the ugly reality of the drawing that she could not quite put out of her mind.

3

IN ELEVENTH GRADE, MARIETTA STOVER had found herself with a curious mixture of pluses and minuses. There was the fact, for instance, that she had the most beautiful face that had ever graced the halls of Winthrop High, a face that suggested to most people Grace Kelly at her youngest and most lovely. But then the minuses took over. Marietta had no breasts to speak of, and her ankles, while not very thick, were not nearly so graceful as her long neck or elegant wrists and fingers. Then there was her reputation, which on the one hand (accurately) billed her as almost too good to be true—the daughter of money who nonetheless was not in any way snobbish and who in fact spent her high school Saturdays not at football games and matinees, but working in the hospital on the ward for the indigent (at the time she had planned, much to her mother's disdain, to go into nursing). On the other hand, she was shy to the point of paralysis and this tended to give the impression of aloofness. Only among the hospital's poor, where she dispensed soup, bandages, and as much good feeling as possible, did she feel secure. She learned, from this expe-

51

rience, that she was happiest only when she had a Project at hand, whether that Project was maintaining a straight A average, helping the new blind student learn her way around the halls of Wintrop High, or helping the choirmaster at the local Lutheran church turn the collection of tone-deaf but very sincere choir members into real singers.

Unfortunately, it was her penchant for Projects that initially got her involved with Glen Stover, at a time in high school when, despite his really striking good looks and his very wealthy family, he was something of a social pariah. Glen was one of those boys who had decided to punish the world for the pain that had been inflicted upon him at a very early age (and twenty minutes with his parents told you all you needed to know—the doting but bullying mother, the arrogant and unfathomably insensitive father). So he was constantly in trouble for smashing windows, stealing cars, getting girls pregnant, smoking marijuana (this several years before Flower Power and all that made marijuana at least arguably respectable), and doing some pretty deadly imitations of his various teachers. By the time she met him senior year, he had twice been expelled from public school, twice sent to military school from which he'd also been expelled, and was living under a court's threat to send him to reform school if he was ever again arrested for going 130 miles per hour in his father's Cadillac convertible (his father owning, among many other businesses, the local Cadillac-Oldsmobile dealership).

Two things happened to make Marietta susceptible to Glen's raw charms. She'd just been thrown over by a very earnest but probably homosexual college freshman painter who had had dreamy blue eyes and the ability to

52

talk endlessly about great art, if not produce it (hard as she'd tried, she'd never quite been able to understand his paintings, they were all sort of a blurry mess to her untutored eyes; nor had she ever been able to coax him into sex, either). And secondly, on the night she danced slow with Glen for the first time (it was to a Bobby Vinton record that she remembered as being "Mr. Lonely" and Glen remembered as "Blue Velvet"), she had just learned that her father had become afflicted with Lou Gehrig's disease, the second member of his family to be struck with the fatal illness. Her socialite mother had gone completely to hell. And so on this night she'd been in search of two things: a friend and a new Project, a Project so impossible on its face, so all-consuming in its demands that there would be no idle time to worry about her father or about what her own future held. Friend and Project came in the same person—Glen Stover. During their very first dance together, he let his hand drop onto her bottom. During their second dance together, there in the darkness of the gym, he forced his tongue into her mouth and pressed their bodies together. During their third dance together, he whispered quite loudly (so that those around them sniggered) what he wished to do with her if only she would accompany him outside. He was quite drunk of course and as boorish as he'd ever been in his life. And during their fourth dance together, she decided to do something about both these unfortunate facts: she slapped him only once, but so jaw-shatteringly hard that he literally shot back into the brick wall. Then she took his hand and yanked him out of the gym. He was crying —whether from shame or rage, she wasn't sure—and babbling. He wanted to know just where she thought she was taking him. He wanted to know just what she

53

thought she was doing. He wanted to know if she thought he wouldn't hit a woman because if she knew any goddamn thing about him, she should know goddamn well that he'd hit a woman any time he felt like it. All she told him before they reached his Oldsmobile was that he should not take the Lord's name in vain. In the car, he would not speak. He sat sullen and still humiliated. Then she slipped over to him and said that if they were going to do this, then they'd better do it well and do it properly. And he'd just said "Do what?" and she'd said, "You mean you really don't know?" And this time it was she who kissed him, putting her tongue in his mouth, and setting one of his big hands on one of her small breasts.

And so that was how it started, and the terrible thing was that it never got any better, not the sex and certainly not the friendship. But she persisted through it all (until the night of her thirty-sixth birthday when she'd caught him screwing this doctor's wife in the garage on a bed of lawn fertilizer bags, his white ass pumping away and the doctor's wife's heel wrapped up somewhere around his neck). But Marietta had married him and bore him two children (both through Caesarean) and only occasionally threatened divorce. And only occasionally admitted to herself that A—their friendship had failed, and B—so had her Project. She had never been able to change him from what he was—a shallow, spoiled, dishonorable little boy, who still made her sad in a way she would never be able to understand.

Her Project now was the household—the girls (Hedley, 6, and Annie, 3) and the house itself, which she redecorated each spring with the enthusiasm of an Egyptian princess designing her pyramid. (This year the living room had been done in Country French, with caned chairs and overstuffed upholstery, a writing desk flown here from Paris, and upstairs canopy beds with full-sized armoires with handcarved scrollwork and shell motifs in warm fruitwood finish.)

Of course, she had to be The Wife, as well, which explained why she was so busy helping Glen with the club's One Hundredth Anniversary and why, now, she was standing at the foot of the stairs listening to her small girls squeal with delight over something the babysitter Glen had brought home was showing them.

She wondered what it was. Her girls were so reserved. Plus they tended on principle to hate all babysitters.

Marietta, dressed this afternoon in faded Big Mac dungarees and a ragged sweatshirt that said SWIM TEAM (one of her last remnants from college) went up the sweeping carpeted stairs to the second landing and then quietly approached Hedley's room, where the three of them were.

The girls' laughter grew more audible the closer she got, and for a moment she felt an irrational pang of jealousy. She could never make her girls laugh this way. Never; no matter how silly or playful she got.

She moved up to the room and peered in.

Three-year-old Annie stood in her jeans and white Smurfs T-shirt and blue Keds. Six-year-old Hedley, dressed in jeans and a white blouse and blue Keds, stood next to her. The age difference wasn't the only way you could tell the girls apart. Annie was white blonde and Hedley auburn-haired.

At first, peering around the corner, she wasn't sure what the girls were doing. Being Hedley's room, the decor featured massive overhead beams painted blue, colonial-style shutters, two large hook rugs that provided earth tone contrast to the flawlessly varnished floor. As the day fell to dusk, deep shadows collected in the corners of the room, casting the teenage girl on the edge of the quilt-covered bed into near darkness.

The two girls held the babysitter's hands, forming a loose circle. None of the three spoke. They simply stared at each other.

"I can feel it!" exclaimed three-year-old Annie. "Inside my head!"

"So can I!" cried Hedley.

Hedley's enthusiasm for the mysterious game surprised Marietta. These days Hedley pretended to a great sophistication. Still, the question was, what exactly were the three of them *doing*?

"All right," the babysitter said (she'd been introduced to Marietta; what was her name—something that could have been a boy's name as well; Leigh? No, Nikki; that was it; Nikki). "All right. Let's keep holding hands and now I'm going to think of something and I want to see if you two can guess it. Okay?"

"Hurry up and think it!" blurted Annie.

Nikki closed her eyes. The girls held hands very tightly. Marietta could see their knuckles straining white from their grips.

All of it—the handholding, the closing of the eyes, the intense stillness—began to remind Marietta of a seance she'd attended on a lark during her senior year in college, during the course of which she did or didn't make contact with a deceased aunt of hers she'd loved madly. The did or didn't depended on whether Marietta needed to believe in the spirit world to get through a particular day. Sometimes you needed the notion of a spirit world to lean on, and sometimes you didn't.

The girls cried out in unison. "You're thinking that tonight we'll watch a movie on the VCR and make red popcorn balls!"

Without quite knowing why, Marietta felt her stomach tighten. A thin layer of sweat broke out on her forehead.

How could both girls have come up with so specific an answer—"red popcorn balls"—when no words, not even any hints, had been exchanged?

Nikki said, "That's very good. Want to try again?"

"Yes!" cried Annie. "Yes!"

Hedley's small, pretty head bobbed up and down in agreement.

"This time, let's let Hedley have the thought, Annie, and then you and I can guess it. Would you like that?"

"Yes!" Annie said again.

But Hedley looked nervous. "Do you really think I can do it?"

"If you just relax and think a very clear thought, you can," Nikki said. Even in the near darkness you could see her white smile. She was a very appealing girl.

"All right," Hedley said. But she still sounded nervous.

Hedley closed her eyes just as Nikki had.

And then Marietta accidentally leaned on a dead board and a creak as loud as a curse sounded in the silent room.

The girls, still holding hands, turned to stare at her, and for the first time Marietta got a good look at their eyes.

There was something different about their gazes, but she couldn't say what exactly. All she knew was that she felt excluded—angrily so—from whatever was going on in Hedley's room.

"Mother," Hedley said. "What are you doing spying on us?"

Marietta felt as helpless and humiliated as she had the night she'd caught her husband in the garage with the doctor's wife.

She started to speak. She wanted to say, *You're my daughters. Why are you looking at me this way?*

But no words came out.

Hedley, looking at Nikki, said, "Let's stop. It's no fun if grown-ups have to be around."

Nikki, soothingly, said, "We're just having some fun, Mrs. Stover." She dropped the girls' hands. "Just having some fun."

Marietta had at last found her voice. She tried to sound commanding. "I'd prefer it if the girls came downstairs and played in the TV room."

Nikki stood up. Came out of the shadows. In the light she looked like an ordinary enough young girl. What had Marietta been expecting? Horns on her head? "Sure, Mrs. Stover." She put her hands on the girls' shoulders. "Why don't we go downstairs now, girls?"

Hedley said, "Thanks very much, mother. We really appreciate your spoiling this for us."

She had never before, not once, used that tone with her mother. Hedley, if anything, was Marietta's pet. Annie, so rambunctious, could tend to fray the nerves. But Hedley was so gentle and soft-spoken . . .

Hedley stormed off down the stairs, leaving Marietta to burst into tears and then flee down the hall to her own room.

She went in and flung herself on the bed. She felt as if she were losing her mind.

What had she seen in the room with the girls? Had

they really been communicating through telepathy? But no, that was impossible, Marietta thought, trying to draw herself together again. She was a strong, sensible, giving woman. She supposed it wasn't the game they'd been playing—though that had certainly disturbed her—but the way Hedley had sassed her and then stormed off. That was the part of the whole incident she'd never forget.

The hatred, the absolute hatred, in Hedley's eyes.

4

"SHE ASLEEP?" DAVID FAIRBAIN ASKED.

"Yes," Jody said.

"She'll be better now."

"I hope so."

"Like a drink?" David said.

She smiled. "There are a lot of years separating us, David. I'm an alcoholic."

"Oh."

"I'm sorry if that puts you on the spot. I mean, it's still sort of an awkward thing for me to admit."

"Well, then maybe I won't have so much trouble telling you about my heart attack."

"God, really. When?" Jody asked.

"Last year about this time. They nearly lost me."

"God."

"To be truthful, they still don't know if I'm going to make it."

Tiny little lines wrinkled her forehead. "You look fine."

"That's one of the problems with myocarditis, I'm afraid. Doctors tend to get it confused with conditions that aren't as serious, and sometimes don't recognize it until it's too late." He smiled. "Still don't know what myocarditis is, eh?"

She laughed. "If this is a pop quiz, I'm failing."

"It's a degenerative disease of the heart muscle. The doctors happened to stumble on it when they were trying to save me from my heart attack. In the old days, myocarditis was usually caused by things such as syphilis and goiter. In my case, it seems to have been caused by hypertension."

She watched him closely as he spoke, seeing the boy she remembered in the man who sat across the living room from her now. He still had that nice, proper presence—a boy well raised—and he still had that slow, killer smile, and he still had those serious blue eyes she'd dreamed of so many grade school nights. But now they were nearly fifty and sitting in the front room of a rental house whose bruised and battered walls gave all indication that the previous occupants had most likely been a gang of Hells Angels out to raise some hell just before they were taken to prison for a long stint.

He had white hair and slightly slouched shoulders and even a few liver spots on his hands, and yet she felt an unmistakable thrill at sitting in his presence again. Perhaps there were some people whose approval you wanted no matter how old you got. David Fairbain seemed to be one of them.

He was shrugging now, sitting back in the overstuffed armchair with the doily on the plump right arm. The doily concealed a huge black cavern of a cigarette burn.

The biker gang had been a busy bunch. "I could live twenty-five more years or I could drop dead tomorrow."

She smiled sadly, not knowing what to say.

"But, as one of my doctors said, that's true of any of us." For the first time, a suggestion of melancholy came into his gaze. "Life's a pretty fragile business, I'm afraid. For all of us."

When he said this, Jody thought of Jenny. Of the terrible destruction she'd visited on Ruth Peary's office. Of the curious transformation that seemed to have taken her over.

"So I quit my job on the *Tribune* and came back here," David went on. "I came into a small inheritance when my folks died and I just decided to spend my time as I really wanted to." He paused and looked out the window. "I'm writing a history of Winthrop. I figure it will take me two years or so to finish, and then the State University press is going to publish it."

"That's wonderful, David."

"Actually, I think it is. I haven't felt this good about myself since—" He paused and once more the impression of melancholy encompassed him like a force field, stronger now than before. "I'm afraid I had a pretty terrible marriage. I used to think it was all her fault, and then I went through a period thinking it was all my fault, and now I'm not so sure." He shook off the mood instantly and said, "But, anyway, I brought up the book for a particular reason."

Jody wanted, naturally enough, to find out more about his marriage. She had the alcoholic's interest in all human disasters, probably because it was encouraging to know that others had suffered, too, and had triumphed over their suffering. But he wanted to discuss his book.

"I've become a good friend of both Doc Coyle and the police chief. They both go back several decades here."

"Yes?" She had no idea where this was leading.

"Well, I just thought I'd do a little checking if you didn't mind."

She was about to ask him about what he meant by "checking" when Samantha appeared.

Sam had gotten the best physical qualities of both Jody and Jody's first husband, a dashing but faithless United pilot who six years after the divorce ended up crashing into the Everglades while guiding a charter plane loaded with insurance executives. She'd always wondered if he'd been sober.

Sam, with her cheekbones and her enigmatic smile and her sloe brown eyes had easily won a place in the lower echelons of New York City modeling. No *Vogue* covers but plenty of work in J.C. Penney catalogs and lots of runway jobs for the mass market designers who imitated to the legal limit the designs of Perry Ellis, Bill Blass, and Ralph Lauren. Unfortunately, along with great looks, an easy sense of humor, a spectacular five-ten body, and a really good mind, she had also inherited her parents' addictive personalities.

She stood now, wan from her latest cocaine run, wearing a red summer cable sweater and jeans, her baby blond hair tumbling down to her shoulders. Even though she wore no makeup, she looked wonderful, and Jody had to admit to two different feelings—pride in a daughter she loved beyond words and a small pang of jealousy at the way David stirred in his chair when he saw her.

"Hi," she said. Then she offered them both her smile. "I have to admit, I kept the bathroom door open and I sort of overheard your conversation." She crossed the dusky room and shook David's hand. "You're David Fairbain. I've been hearing about you all my life."

Her mother laughed. "Thanks for all the help."

"I mean, I assume," Sam said, "that you know the kind of crush my mother used to have on you. We're talking major heartbreak, right, Mom?"

David smiled but looked a bit embarrassed. He was not completely easy around women, and Jody found herself liking him for that. She'd had a lifetime of glib men and their lines.

"Anyway," Sam said, more seriously. "I really am glad to meet you."

It was during these periods, completely away from drugs, completely resolved to never take drugs again, that Jody and Sam rediscovered their old relationship, the one that had bloomed in Sam's late teen years when Jody had joined Alcoholics Anonymous and begun, for the first time, to really be a mother.

Sam came over and sat down next to her on the couch. "How did it go with the shrink and Jenny?"

Jody felt herself tense. She cleared her throat.

Sam, who knew her too well to be misled, obviously sensed right away that something was wrong. She said, with surprising calm, "What happened?"

"We're not sure."

"Mom, please just tell me."

Jody cleared her throat again. "She—threw some kind of fit. That's all I can say."

"Some kind of *fit*? I don't understand."

"She became violent. Overturned furniture. Tried to slap Dr. Peary."

"Jenny? My little daughter?" Now her voice was rising. Now her voice reflected concern and perhaps even panic. She licked dry lips. "And we don't know what caused it?"

"Jenny hinted that something happened the other night."

"The other night? Did she say which night?"

"No." Jody thought of telling her about the strange drawing, the hideous thing she recalled from her own girlhood. But she decided that would only make things worse. She said, "Were you with Jenny all the time the past few days?"

"Yes." Then she shook her head. "All but three nights ago." She flushed, glanced at David. "I—" She shrugged. "I went out one night with some people I met downtown. I left Jenny with a babysitter."

For some reason, her mention of a babysitter seemed to interest David as much as it did Jody.

"What did the babysitter say when you got home?" Jody asked.

"Well," Sam began hesitantly. "To tell the truth—" She paused again. Sighed. "To tell the truth, I was pretty wrecked. I remember paying her exorbitantly and I remember her leaving. That's about all."

"And Jenny didn't say anything to you?"

"No."

"Nothing about anything going wrong?"

"No. Nothing that I can remember."

"How was she the next day?"

"Fine but—" Then she stopped. "No, wait a minute. The next night I heard her crying, really sobbing. I assumed it was because I'd been out the night before. She knows me well enough to know when I go back on the— stuff. I just assumed she was crying because she knew what I'd done."

David said, "You didn't happen to write down the name of the babysitter, did you?"

"I might have it somewhere," Sam said. "Why?"

"Maybe it would help to talk to her."

"That sounds like a good idea," Jody said, still curious about David's sudden interest in the babysitter.

Sam said, "Why all the interest in the babysitter?" She sounded both vaguely irritated and vaguely upset by the idea.

"I just thought that she could help us know what happened here that night—if something did," David said. "It just seems an orderly way to proceed."

Jody took Sam's hand. Whenever Sam was coming off a drug binge, she was first physically sick and then mentally unstable. Her reactions were not unlike those of premenstrual syndrome—great anxiety and depression crossed with an almost chronic inability to relax. Jody said, "He's just trying to help, hon."

Sam visibly relaxed then. "Sorry I got cranky."

"That was cranky? You should work on a newspaper sometime," David said. "Then you'll know what cranky is."

Sam smiled. "Or be around my mother when she hasn't had enough sleep."

Jody patted Sam's hand again. "Time for family secrets now?" She stood up. "I'll call Iris Manners and get the babysitter's name from her. You just stay here and talk with David."

With that, Jody left the living room, walked through the small, empty dining room with its tanned, stained carpet crying out for a cleaning, and then into the kitchen where a yellow wall phone rested against a bright red wall. The people who had owned this house before it was a rental must have been color blind.

As she dialed, she looked over at the wobbly kitchen table with the cardboard box full of picnic supplies—paper plates, plastic forks, paper place mats—and she felt again an abiding pity for her daughter. Sam still lived this way, rarely with a stable man around, even more rarely in any one particular place for any length of time. She was always changing apartments and small rental houses on the outskirts of New York City, always trying to find somewhere outside her own heart for that sense of peace she had sought so desperately and for so long.

The kitchen window was cracked. Behind it the screen had been pulled away and hung dangling and rusty. A loud wasp slammed against the window. Far off Jody could hear the roar of Interstate 80, and even further off the clatter of a fast train.

On the sixth ring, Iris Manners answered. Iris had been one of Jody's favorite classmates, a plump woman with a yen for the kitchen and raising very well-behaved children, and an absolute indifference to the opinion of other people.

"Hello."

"Hi, Iris, it's me. Jody."

"Say, do I have some news for you," Iris said, before Jody could even get a word out about the reason she'd called.

"You do?"

"Fred Phillips saw you at the store today. You remember Fred?"

"Sort of."

"He was in our class and he's now the swim coach at the high school."

"Oh. Right. Fred."

"Well, you should have heard what he said about you."

She'd never been able to accept compliments well, so now Jody giggled like a girl and said, "Something pretty bad, huh?"

"Well, in case you don't know, he keeps himself in very good shape not only swimming but lifting weights, *and* he's a widower. And he wanted to know if I'd sort of reintroduce you."

"Well, that's nice."

"Boy, you really sound excited, Jody." She laughed. "I guess when you look like I do, you'd just naturally go a little crazy if anybody had an illicit thought about you at all. And I think ole Fred had a *lot* of illicit thoughts about you." Now it was Iris of the dishwater hands and six children who was doing the giggling. She said, "You didn't actually have a reason to call me, did you?"

Jody grew serious. "I'm afraid I did, Iris."

"Something wrong?" Iris said, sensing her mood at once.

"I'm afraid there is."

"Sam?"

"No. Jenny."

"Jenny? My God."

"She had some sort of—spell this afternoon. Got very upset when we took her to see Dr. Peary."

"Oh, yes. I've heard good things about her. The Emersons went to her when Jan Emerson was seeing that fellow from Center City. Mike Emerson always likes to say that Ruth Peary saved his marriage. Jan gave up the Center City fellow, at any rate."

"I had a good impression of her, too."

"So what about Jenny?"

"Well, apparently she told Ruth Peary that something happened the other night. I just wondered if you knew the number of the babysitter you recommended to Sam."

"Oh, Gol, Jody, you think that babysitter did something?"

"Do you know this girl?"

"Not real well. Agnes Thorp recommended her to me, actually. I couldn't think of anybody for Sam so I called Agnes and I got this girl's number."

"Do you have it written down?"

Jody could hear Iris leaning away from the phone. "Let me see if I still have it on this little blackboard I keep over by the refrigerator. Just a minute." She put the phone down. Jody could hear walking-away footsteps. In a few moments, Iris was back. "Just be grateful that I never clean this dump up," she laughed. "Here's the number." She gave it to her and said, "How's Jenny doing now?"

"As soon as I hang up, I'm going to go in and check on her. But you don't know anything about this girl, then?"

"Sorry. Wish I did. All I know is that Agnes used her once and said she was reliable." She coughed and then said, "Remember how we used to compete for babysitting jobs? How much we wanted to make twenty-five cents an hour? These kids today—" She stopped herself. "Gol, don't I sound like those old biddies we used to hate? 'These kids today.' Like Mrs. Crumb. Remember Mrs. Crumb and how much she used to hate 'new-fangled kids,' as she liked to put it?"

A vivid image of a gnarled old woman filled Jody's mind. "Her and her walking stick and her Camel cigarettes."

"Smoked more than any man I ever knew. And what a bitch. Pardon my French."

"Yes, Iris, that is a pretty shocking word."

"I forgot. You're from the big city now. You probably use the F word and everything."

"You mean you never do?"

"Not so's I'd admit it."

Jody laughed, liking Iris all the more. "You're a good friend, Iris, and I appreciate your help."

"Well, you try that number and see if you have any luck."

"Thanks, again."

"My pleasure, hon. I just hope you're still planning to have lunch with me before you leave."

"You promise not to bring Fred Phillips along?"

"How much will you pay me?"

"Bye, hon," Jody said sweetly, and hung up the phone.

She immediately dialed the number Iris had given her. She could tell from the connecting ring that something was wrong with the line. On the third ring a recorded voice said, "The number you have dialed is no longer in service. If you wish assistance, please stay on the line."

Jody opted to stay on the line.

After a minute or so an operator came on. "May I help you?"

Jody gave her the number. "Is there a forwarding number?"

"If there was," the operator said pleasantly, "it would be on the recording."

"Oh." Then she said, "Do you have any way of telling me the address of this phone number?"

"I'm sorry. We're not permitted to do that."

"I see."

Now the operator had grown impatient. "Is there any other way I can help you?"

"I guess not. Thanks."

After replacing the phone, Jody went down the hall, first to the bathroom where she peed. Then she washed up, freshened her lipstick and started back down the hall to Jenny's room.

She sensed immediately that something was wrong because the door stood ajar. Then she decided she was being paranoid. Maybe Jenny had gotten up and gone to the bathroom and then gone back to bed, leaving the door partially open on her way back.

Jody looked inside. The room was bare except for a small, lumpy roll-away bed. A few dresses hung in the otherwise empty closet. A happy teddy bear sat on the floor next to a scratched-up bureau. The place had been advertised as "furnished." That was employing a very liberal interpretation of that word.

Jody went immediately to the living room. What she hoped to do was round the corner and find Jenny sitting there on the couch with Sam.

Jenny was not in the living room.

Jody's panic must have been pretty transparent. Within seconds of each other, both Sam and David asked what was wrong.

"I just wondered if you'd seen Jenny," Jody said, trying to sound calm and casual.

But it was too late for calm and casual.

Having sensed Jody's concern, Sam and David were on their feet. They each began searching the house with a distinct air of desperation.

It quickly became clear that eight-year-old Jenny was gone.

5

IF YOU LIVED AROUND WINTHROP AND drove Interstate 80 virtually any time of year, you saw James. Almost nobody knew his name except the occasional police officer who stopped him and asked to see some ID, or the even more occasional citizen who struck up a conversation.

His skin was the sunburnt color of the Mesquakie Indians who lived on a shabby reservation sixty miles to the east in the piney hills that had been strip-mined out about the time Eisenhower was warning us about the military-industrial complex. His gray hair and imposing dark gaze provided sharp contrast to his red skin, and the unfailing step of his gait spoke of a much younger man. Presumably he was well over sixty, though you couldn't tell for sure.

He mostly spent the day walking the grassy strip between the opposing lanes of Interstate 80 looking for pop and beer cans. He always carried a huge, dirty Hefty bag which, by day's end, looked like a swollen brown plastic animal. He always took the cans to the same supermarket where the teenagers working the cash register generally regarded him with an uneasy mixture of contempt and fear. But it wasn't just the teenagers who regarded him this way. He was a man who made nearly everybody uncomfortable. Perhaps it was his silence. Perhaps it was the stubborn enigmatic glare of his gaze. Perhaps it was his calloused outsized hands, hands that looked perfect for being wrapped around a white throat. (The local Indians evoked a curious ambiguity in white people—in equal parts they pitied and despised them.) For a full bag of cans he got $5.50. He stayed until they started staring at him. With part of the proceeds he generally bought two items, a package of generic filter cigarettes and a full can of Pepsi which he took down in two or three impressive gulps. Then he would be gone. Few knew where he lived. Fewer cared.

Now, at the end of this day, he left the supermarket with his cigarettes and Pepsi and began the return to wherever he lived. Today, as usual, he walked alleys instead of streets. Teenagers hassled him sometimes and he avoided hassles as much as possible, which was why he always suffered silently the indignities of the young police officers who felt compelled to ask him for ID, even though he was doing nothing illegal and obviously not bothering anybody. He just looked suspicious. There was the matter of his skin. There was the matter of his silence. There was the matter of his gaze. Even seen from a passing car he made people nervous. White people.

Today he took a quarter from his Hefty bag proceeds (the bag now folded and stuck neatly in his right back pocket along with the billfold that contained his food stamps and his Medicare card) and did something he rarely did because he did not like spending the money. He stopped on the edge of a DX station and went into the phone booth and placed a call.

He said, "There will be a girl there tonight."

The woman on the other end of the phone sighed. "There is a lot of noise in the basement. I assumed somebody would be coming." She paused. "Someday they will find out."

"It is not something I like. You know that." He spoke in a curious, broken English. When he was a boy on the reservation he had always ducked out of school and roamed the land to go fishing, and to roam the hills where wildflowers and deer made him forget entirely the harsh ways of his white captors. Nights, he listened to the old ones recall the days when there had been no white people at all in this land, when Mesquakie villages bloomed on the plains, and when song could be heard around the communal fires beneath the splendid stars. The old ones always quoted the Sauk Chief Black Hawk who had said, the day he was sent to the reservation: "If a prophet had come to our village in those days and told us that the things were to take place which have since come to pass, none of our people would have believed him." But even back in the twenties, when he was a boy, things had been better than now. At least the water was blue before the chemicals had been dumped downriver, and the hills had been an unending green before the strip-mining, and the rate of alcoholism and suicide on the reservation was but a fraction of what it was now.

Into the phone, he said, "I do not do this by choice."

The woman sighed. "I know."

"If the Creator would show me a way—"

Again the woman sighed. "How do you know there will be a girl tonight?"

"Last night I could not sleep. I sat at the window and watched the stars. Sometime after midnight I heard the noise in the basement. After such noise, there is always a girl."

"I won't go down there."

"I understand."

"The time you were sick, you wanted me to lead the one girl down the steps. I'm telling you, I won't do it."

"I know."

She paused. "James, this is not right."

He looked around at the fine, shiny cars of the white

people, the Buicks and Oldsmobiles and the imported sports cars, how they flashed in the streetlights, like fish swimming fast in the clear waters of yesterday. He said, "We will talk about this later."

The woman made an unpleasant sound. "The basement again. I'm afraid."

"I will be there soon."

"How soon?"

"I am near downtown. I will be there within twenty minutes."

"I'll be outside in the garden, then."

"It is too dark for the garden."

"I'll just stand there and listen to the animals in the night, then."

He said, feeling sorry for her, "You know what will happen to our own daughter if we do not obey."

"But all the little girls—"

"Do you remember the face of our daughter?"

The woman cursed. "You should not have helped that woman that time—"

He cut her off with his own curse. "She was one of our own. From the reservation." But he spoke here with a curious lack of fire. It had been so long ago. His hair had been black then, and he had still believed in the precepts of the socialist meetings he always attended at a nearby university. Now his hair was gray and soon enough the grave would claim him and he believed in nothing. "It was long ago," he said. "I will be home soon."

Before he could hang up, she said, "I don't want to see the girl."

"What?"

"When she comes tonight, I don't want to see her. I

don't want to hear her." She paused. "I think I'll go into town."

He knew what that meant. It was a code between them. She would go to a tavern and drink the cheap tap beer the whites charged fifty cents a glass for, and she would listen to country music on the jukebox, and she would get very teary and sorry for herself. She would drink this way until it was time to go outside in the moonlight and vomit on the green bushes. Then, scarcely able to form coherent words, she would wobble to a phone booth and call him and cry and say how afraid everything made her, but especially the basement. He would come and get her and let her lean on him and together they would go back home. The white workers who drank late always saw most of this. It was one of the stories they most liked to laugh about. In these parts there were a lot of tales about the crazed reservation Indians, particularly those too proud to live on government land.

But he had to let her go to the tavern at least once a month because she had the same sickness her father and brother had had. Her father, drunk and badly in need of a drink, had mistaken bleach for beer. He had vomited up gouty knots of blood before they could get him to the emergency room in town. He had died with his legs and arms twitching so violently that even the doctor had winced at the sight.

"Yes," he said, now. "Perhaps tonight would be a good night for the tavern."

Once, long ago, when she was young and slender and still very beautiful, she had gone to a tavern and left in a white man's car. She had been so drunk that she could not recall exactly what had happened. But he had always assumed the worst, that she had given herself to the white man. But much of this he attributed to the basement and what had happened to their daughter, and the fact that it was genuinely all of his own doing, even though he had not known what would happen when he'd simply offered to help the woman . . .

Never again had his wife given herself to another, so he did not begrudge her those tavern nights. He supposed she derived from them the same satisfaction he did in climbing the clay hills in autumn . . . when the trees were on fire and the air was filled with the smell of burning leaves, and it was easy to imagine on the plains below the sight of calico horses at full gallop beneath the wailing bodies of war-painted Mesquakie braves . . .

His wife was crying now. She always cried. "Will you talk to her tonight?"

He did not have to ask to whom she was referring. "Yes," he said. "When the girl comes and I have to take her downstairs. Then I will talk to her."

"Tell her I love her."

"She knows that."

The bitterness was back. It cracked like a whip. "If you had not helped that woman that time—"

He hung up.

There were times he could not face what had taken place in his basement.

She was right, his wife. If he had not helped that woman . . .

He found shadows quickly, the shadows of alleys, and finally the shadows of a gravel road stretching white in the light of the quarter moon clear into the country, winding up into the thick green hills where his shack of tin and board sat in a small gully protected by a perfect encirclement of scrub pines.

The guilt was back with him. The guilt was the worst thing of all.

He saw his daughter's face as a little girl, felt again her soft moist little-girl kisses on his cheek.

Once the woman had come and he had helped her—afterward his daughter was never the same again . . .

Never . . .

There in the shadows, alone, a red man with gray hair, he let roll down his gaunt cheeks the silver tears of remorse . . .

Chapter Three

THEY STARTED BY ASKING THE NEAREST neighbors if any of them had seen Jenny. Because Sam and Jenny had been here for about three weeks, most of the neighbors had no idea what the eight-year-old looked like.

After turning up nothing in this manner, they explored a shallow wooded area to the east of the house. Jody and Sam had flashlights. David carried a rake with which he combed the thick brush of bloodroot, ginseng, wild ginger, and berry.

By this time, half an hour after discovering the girl gone, the three of them were hoarse from shouting her name. Sam had started sobbing so much that the other two had to stop and just hold her until the tears abated, at least for the time.

Then it was onward into the shallow woods, heat,

darkness, and mosquitos making their passage uncertain and somewhat difficult.

On the ground, their flashlights picked out beer cans, candy wrappers, pages torn from magazines, and sleek red Trojan wrappers. But no sign of a little girl. No sign whatsoever.

"Hank, this is David Fairbain." He spoke from the kitchen of Sam's rental house.

"Hello, David." The Winthrop Police Chief cupped the phone a moment and asked his wife to turn down the TV set. "How're you doing?"

"Not too well at the moment, I'm afraid."

"Oh?"

"I'm afraid we've got a missing child on our hands."

"Oh." He offered this second "Oh" with much more concern in his voice.

"You remember Jody, don't you?"

"Sure. One of the prettiest girls in our class."

"Well, it's her granddaughter, Jenny."

"How old is she?"

"Eight."

"How long she been gone?"

"About an hour now."

"You've checked with the neighbors?"

"Yes. We've even done a little exploring into a woods close by. Nothing."

"Any evidence of violence around the house?"

"I'm afraid I don't follow you?"

"Any indication she was abducted?"

"No. Somehow she just got out the back door. I checked the window in her bedroom and it doesn't show signs of tampering inside or outside. And if she'd tried to get out the front door, we would have seen her."

"She having any disagreement with her parents?"

"She's here with her mother. And yes, she has been upset, but I'm not sure that has any bearing here."

"Well, a lot of time we find that kids between her age and twelve have disputes with their parents and wander off for a little while." Chief Carella seemed to be offering the hope, however slender, that this might not be so dire a moment as it seemed. "And they always show up soon after. They start hearing the stray dogs barking and seeing how dark it gets at night, and they get scared and come back."

David Fairbain, leaning against the wall in Sam's kitchen, said, "I'm not so sure, Hank."

"Well, whatever's going on, I'm going to send a car out there right now."

"I'd appreciate that, Hank. And there's one more thing I'd like to ask."

"Sure."

"Do you have a book that will tell me what address belongs with a certain phone number?"

"At the station, yes."

"All right with you if I call there and tell them I have your permission to use the book?"

"No problem. Ask for an officer named Malley."

"Malley. Fine. I appreciate it."

"This number have anything to do with the missing girl?"

"Probably not. Something happened the other night and we'd just like to get all the details."

"You're not sure what happened you mean?"

"Right. The only two people who could tell us are Jenny and the babysitter."

"The babysitter is who you're trying to locate?"

"Right."

"You want me to help?"

"No, I thought I'd drive over there when I got the address and just do a little checking around myself. But I would appreciate it if you'd send that car out so we can get a description of Jenny on TV and radio. In case somebody sees her."

"We've got a 'Childwatch' deal on both the local TV stations. Why don't you or Jody call in the description right away. They'll put it right on."

"Good idea. Thanks, Hank."

"No problem. Just tell Jody that I'm sure everything's all right and that we'll find her granddaughter."

He thanked Hank again, hung up, and went back into the living room.

Sam sat like a child huddled in her mother's arms. The small, shadowy light glowing from the tiny brass table lamp cast the two women in a soft color that resembled a Vermeer painting.

He came in quietly. He said nothing. He sat in a chair across from them and waited until Jody was finished stroking her daughter's hair. Gently, gently. It was like trying to get an overtired small child to sleep. You had to be very patient and loving.

David Fairbain tried not to think of his own son he saw so seldom . . .

Finally, when Sam had fallen into a troubled sleep, he helped Jody carry her into the bedroom and stretch her out on the bed.

"I gave her a sleeping pill," Jody said. "I'm just afraid

she's not strong enough to handle this." She frowned. "This is a very bad point for an addict."

The bedroom looked like the rest of the house. The walls were done in a gaudy pastel, plaster was chipped from the ceiling, and a light socket hung askew.

They stood over Sam, looking down at her as if she were their child.

David said, "Hank seems to think Jenny will show up on her own."

"I wish I shared his optimism."

David sighed. "I wish I did, too."

He asked for Officer Malley and was immediately turned over to a man who sounded as if he smoked four or five packs of cigarettes a day.

He explained to Officer Malley what he wanted and Malley said just a minute.

When he came back, after less than a minute, David heard him drop a plump book on the counter or desk or whatever it was and then begin fanning through pages.

All the time he was panting like a man starved for oxygen. In the middle of his search, a paper match exploded. David heard Malley lighting a cigarette.

"Here we go," Malley said. "187 Bridge Street."

"That shouldn't be too tough."

"Well, good luck with the little girl."

"Thanks."

"They usually turn up, you know."

"That's what Hank says."

Malley, coughing, said, "He's right, too. They usually turn up slick as hell."

"Thanks again."

The Babysitter

* * *

The two uniformed officers, both with bands of sweat around the light blue armpits of their uniform shirts, both with squeaking leather holsters for their Magnums, asked many of the same questions Hank had asked.

After giving both the officers diet Pepsis, Jody began to tell them everything she could think of about Jenny. When she told them about Jenny's behavior in Dr. Peary's office this afternoon, they got particularly curious.

The beefy one with the prematurely graying hair was Hanrahan. He said, "What did Dr. Peary make of all this?"

"That she was disturbed."

"But she didn't give any specific reason as to why?"

"Not really. She thought it might have something to do with the other night."

"The other night?" This came from Krenkel. He looked something like a stereotypical accountant. Thin, with heavy eyebrows, and a somewhat prissy mouth, he said, "What about the other night?"

Jody shrugged. David noted how elegantly she moved. In grade school she'd been a tomboy. "That's the big mystery. We don't *know* what happened the other night. Nobody does except Jenny, and she won't tell us."

David almost reminded Jody that the babysitter knew, too, but stopped himself.

Hanrahan sipped gratefully at his cold diet Pepsi, made a kind of TV commercial "Ah" sound, and said, "We're going to look around the house."

"Do you really think she could just show up?" Jody sounded almost plaintive.

Hanrahan, obviously believing that keeping hope alive

was the best sedative of all under these circumstances, said, "We had a little girl just three weeks ago. Wandered away, got lost, and then was picked up by a delivery man who brought her straight back home."

"So you think—?"

"Absolutely," Hanrahan said. "She'll probably come strolling in very soon now."

"But just to be on the safe side," his partner said, "we'll start checking out the neighborhood. Just in case something turns up."

Both officers downed their soft drinks and stood up. Their gunleather creaked. They looked imposing and somehow wrong—almost menacing—in the shadowy light of the drab living room.

"Thank you," Jody said.

"Thanks for the Pepsi," Krenkel said.

Hanrahan, carrying a silver flashlight the size of a small baseball bat, led the way to the front door.

They nodded and left.

For a long moment, Jody stood frozen at the door, looking like a father-deserted child. Her grief was something David could feel tangibly all the way across the room.

Jody, in barely a whisper, said, "They're not going to find her. They're going to try because they're good men, but they're not going to find her."

Then she was sobbing.

David went to her. At first it was awkward, sliding his arms around her middle and letting her come gently into his embrace.

Her tears were warm and wet against his face as she began hugging him so tightly it was almost painful.

"I just wish I understood what was going on here," she

said. "Why Jenny acted that way this afternoon, and why she ran away."

Then she began crying again. She felt frail in his arms. She smelled of perfume and the day's heat. He reached up and cupped the back of her head with one of his large, purposeful hands and brought her face to his neck.

After a time of silence, of her just holding him, he led her over to the couch and helped her lie down, just as they'd both helped Sam into bed earlier.

He began stroking her cheeks and then her hair. She closed her eyes and he could see exhaustion working its way through her body. Tension was starting to drain her completely.

He said, "I'm going to do a little checking on the babysitter."

"Why don't I go with you?"

"Somebody has to be here when the police come back."

"Oh. Yes." By now her voice was fuzzy with her weariness.

"You can probably get a little nap, which will help you, and by that time, I'll be back."

"Did you find something out about her?"

He explained how Hank's man had helped him locate the address.

"Maybe she'll be able to help us." The plaintive tone was back in Jody's voice.

"Yes. Maybe she will."

Then she drifted off with the quick finality of a child falling asleep.

He leaned over and kissed her once softly on the forehead.

* * *

"You're a lucky man," the doctor had told him on the night of his heart attack, that night being the dividing line in David Fairbain's life. He would never again be the same man, and in some ways that was good, and in some ways that was bad.

After leaving Winthrop for four years of college at the state university, and then being drafted and serving a year in Nam (he had no war stories; he'd worked in supply in a safe office in a massive concrete building in the center of Saigon), he came back to the Midwest, choosing Chicago, where he decided the only thing he could do with his English degree (teachers then being paid even less than now) was to go into public relations ("Write a little copy and kiss a lot of ass" as his first employer had always been fond of saying).

It was during his tenure with his third firm, PR agencies going in and out of business with turnstile frequency, that he met his wife Susan, who also wrote copy as a means of supporting herself. He had done what he usually did with beautiful women—fallen immediately and dangerously in love. He had long ago realized the shabby truth about himself—that he was one of those clinging, dependent, jealous men whom women (whatever their protests to the contrary, however "sensitive" they found the type) despised. Of course, even though every reasonable judgment found them not only incompatible but potentially very destructive as a couple, they had gotten married in one of those ceremonies of the early 70s, designed to somehow deny the fact that this was a marriage ceremony at all. The minister (a Unitarian who later on smoked as many joints as any of the other guests and who said a very loud and liberated "fuck" far oftener

86

than most) read from Gibran, Rod McKuen, and Bob Dylan—words from the Bible being obviously for slobs who drank beer and went bowling in gaudy yellow shirts and who voted for Richard M. Nixon. (One of David's friends remarked that the only writer who hadn't been read by the minister was Kafka.) The wedding night had been no better because, however much they tried to deny the fact, their sex life was pretty bad. She did not like oral sex (his or hers) and he was not especially enamored of all the mutual masturbation she found so exciting. They fell asleep in each other's arms with her telling him that she had not changed her mind: there would be no children.

But a child, inadvertently and unhappily, had come along in the third year of their marriage (she had stormed their apartment for a full week, alternately sobbing and cursing, "I just don't know what could have happened!") and for the first and only time in their lives together, David became so angry that he struck her, a glancing slap on her cheek. The baby, he said, would not be aborted. They were thirty-five goddamn years old, and the years now were going too fast and their lives, from what he could see, were little more than the nightmare their generation had so happily created for itself—endless arcane debates about the rights of women, the rights of men, good sex, bad sex, black and white, straight and gay, accountability to one's spouse, the freedom to do what one chose despite marital bonds, liberation, and principle over passion even if the principle was as ugly as 800,000 aborted fetuses a year.

There would be no goddamn abortion.

Ultimately, she had deferred to him, though he'd had the sense, that she was simply renting him the use of her body to birth the child he wanted so badly, and that the cost of such a rental would be nothing less than the demise of their marriage.

Six months after delivery of the boy they'd named Jerred (that spring Jerred was running a close second to Chad as the preferred name for boys), Susan took the first of a series of lovers and she made little if any attempt to disguise this fact. David had gone insane in the way only jealousy can make one insane. He'd had the sentimental hope that Jerred would turn her into a more traditional wife and mother, but it seemed to have the opposite effect. To make things worse, the recession came and David's small agency, heavily dependent on oil money (how many lies he'd told the public about the good great intentions of the misunderstood oil barons; how much ass he'd kissed) folded, and he became a forerunner of the househusband, a job he liked more than he dared admit to either himself or his wife. Contrarily, her job fortunes soared. She became account manager in an ad agency and took over a huge cosmetics brand that was just then going international (thanks to the intercession of a quiet but socially ambitious mafioso who made sure that the brand would be going into England, France, Spain, and Italy within three months of each other).

That autumn she also managed to infect both of them with clap, a singularly inelegant turn that made his demands of seeing a marriage counselor at last persuasive. He had to admit that she did seem to give the counselor her best honest effort. He also had to admit that during the course of their seventeen sessions he saw for the first time just what a wretched mate he'd been to her—a whining, overly dependent, moralizing twit who far too well reflected his fundamentalist religious upbringing in the smalltown Midwest. For the first time ever, he heard Susan cry tears that seemed genuine, and saw, for the first time ever, that if she had never quite loved him in the way he needed to be loved, she had nonetheless truly cared for him. He also learned how much she loved Jerred; just as much as he did. And he saw, finally, what most mates see at the splitting point—that each contributed more than the necessary share to tear apart the marriage.

As a consequence to all this, they had never been better friends than the day they stood outside the divorce court, both of them teary, both of them hugging. She was moving to Los Angeles to live with the doctor she'd met. Being unemployed, David was in no shape to take Jerred. He surprised himself by feeling comfortable with her taking Jerred for the foreseeable future, even though he knew how devastatingly lonely he would be without his son.

Three months later, unable to take it any longer, David moved to Los Angeles, lucked out in finding a job with an agency that handled a national funeral home association (and finding that funeral home directors, for all their bad press, were the best clients he'd ever worked with; all copy and no ass-kissing) and began spending every other weekend with Jerred. He even became reasonably good friends with Jerred's new stepfather.

There were women, of course, but hard as he tried he could not find within himself any emotion stronger than lust. He sensed that he needed a long period of loneliness to purge himself of the shortcomings that had helped bring down his first marriage.

Then, suddenly, Jerred was fourteen years old and he had his own friends and spending weekends with Dad was not so much fun and, equally suddenly, David found himself beginning to worry about such matters as pension and retirement and finding another woman to marry.

And then one night he'd had his heart attack in the vestibule of his apartment house and all David could say in the ambulance with the round face of the paramedic constantly hanging over his face, was, "Am I going to die?"

But it was also then that he realized the question was somewhat moot. Fearing death presumes that one has good reasons to go on living, and in the white hospital days that followed, he discovered how few were the things that gave him pleasure, how angry he was inside, how ill-equipped he was to understand happiness.

And so, a year later, surviving on a decent-sized savings account, he came back to his hometown and threw himself into writing a history of that hometown.

And then today he'd seen Jody, a girl he'd always noticed, but for some reason never pursued in his younger days . . .

Now he turned his new Chevrolet right onto Swanson Avenue and watched the good two-story middle-class homes give way to a neighborhood that resembled a war zone: windows smashed, the dead carcasses of ancient cars filling front yards, loud and angry husband-wife arguments floating on the air like sad music, and young men and women sitting on stoops and staring out at him with a mixture of scorn and bafflement. How did a guy get a new Chevrolet anyway . . .

It was in this neighborhood that the babysitter had lived. Now he was more curious about her than ever.

He looked at the address on the piece of white scratch paper and slowed down.

She lived in a Gothic monstrosity of gingerbreading, dormer windows, and a widow's walk. Not even the night could hide the condition of the place, the weeds that grew knee-high on the front lawn, the rusty bicycles and barrels and bedsprings strewn across the front porch.

For the first time, he felt some small fear about getting involved in all this.

He had never been a strong man—nor a particularly brave one. And middle-age and a heart condition did not exactly inspire him with self-confidence. He had no idea what he would find . . .

He got out of the car. After the coolness of the Chevrolet's crisp air-conditioning, the night was muggy. Sweat quickly pasted his shirt to his back. Rock and roll blared from a window; another domestic battle was in progress; a motorcycle revved up somewhere in the shadows.

He went up to the front door.

A plump black tomcat sat with a partially eaten mouse in front of it. Serious green eyes raised to meet David's as he squinted at the battered and once gold mailboxes, looking for any identification on apartment No. 6. There was nothing.

Up on the porch the air smelled of spaghetti and beer and cigarette smoke. And filth. Peering into the vestibule, he saw a massive garbage can overflowing with rotten food. Flies buzzed around it in furious circles.

Gulping, he went inside, trying to pay no attention to the garbage can.

Once the octagonal-shaped vestibule had no doubt been fashionable, with parquet flooring and stained glass windows. But the parquet pattern was lost beneath decades of wear and filth and a long gash of stained glass had been smashed out.

He went up the stairs, toward the blare of rock and roll coming from the second floor. On the whitewashed wall paralleling the banister, graffiti of all sorts had been spray-painted. A few words had been written in lipstick that eerily resembled dried blood. He had seen a clever TV movie once about urban vampires. If such creatures existed, this was no doubt the type of place in which they'd hide.

The rock and roll became overpowering by the time he reached the narrow hallway of the second floor. The only illumination was from two dim bulbs spaced ten feet apart and hanging naked from the ceiling. Far down the hall, on either side, were at least a half dozen apartment doors.

Head beginning to throb from the music, stomach gnarled because of the relentless odors, he started walking past doors until he came to No. 6.

Even if someone were inside, he wondered, how would they hear his knock above the music?

He knocked anyway and followed up by pressing his right ear to the door and filling his left ear with a finger so he could cut down the noise.

Nothing.

He was not surprised.

He moved back on down the hall to the apartment from which the rock and roll roared. Shaking his head, he raised his hand and brought it down on the door.

Unlocked, the door swung open and he found himself staring into a wide front room that was lighted only by a small lamp on the floor. The lamp bulb was red and it painted everything in the room that color. Once again, he was reminded of blood.

On the floor, next to the lamp, sat an old man with his

back pressed to the wall. He wore a sleeveless T-shirt. His aged flesh hung loose. Skinny as he was, he had breasts like a young girl's. He raised a head so completely bald it looked shaved, and stared directly at David. He wore sunglasses. He grinned. He had no teeth. He picked up a quart of Hamms beer he kept at his left side and took a huge swig. He grinned toothlessly again and offered the quart to David. Then he beckoned David inside.

For the second time in less than five minutes, David felt great reluctance about being in this house.

He went inside, anyway.

The place was furnished with an overstuffed couch, a small mattress on the floor, and a wobbly card table on which sat a hotplate and a greasy pizza box. White stuffing daubed red by the lamp stuck out of various curves in the couch, reminding David of wounds.

Now that he was closer to the old man, David realized the truly remarkable thing about him. He was covered, nearly entirely, with tattoos. But they were so faded that David had not been able to see them until he came close up. The tattoos were fading from the old man just as his life force was.

David's eyes moved right, and there on the orange crate he saw the stereo. It was a small and beaten Sears model. It was astonishing it could put out so much volume.

David, without asking permission, went over and turned it off.

When he turned back around, he saw that the old man held a switchblade in his hand. With surprisingly deft fingers, the old man released the blade. There was a *snick* sound.

"Don't believe I asked you to turn it down, asshole."

"I need to ask you a few questions."

"You don't scare me none. Not none at all." He paused, his birdlike, paranoid eyes searching the doorway. "You a cop?"

"I look like one?"

"That's bullshit."

"What is?"

"That cops look a certain way. I know cops who look like insurance men and I know cops who look like fairy boys."

"I'm not a cop."

"Then what the fuck are you doin' turnin' down my stereo?"

"Look," David said. "I'm sorry about your stereo, all right? But we're looking for a little girl and right now we need all the help we can get."

For the first time, fear came into the old man. "I don't know nothin' about no little girl. Kids ain't my bag. Just because I did a little time back in Illinois—" He paused, looked at the four-inch blade. The red bulb cast a huge silhouette of his hand and the shiv on the wall behind him.

"Why don't you put the knife away? I'm not saying you know anything about the little girl at all. I just want to ask you a few questions about somebody who lived here."

"Who?"

"A young girl who did babysitting." Before the old man could speak, David said, "The knife. All right?"

"I can git it out again fast, fucker. You remember that."

"I'll remember. I'll remember."

The old man ceremoniously closed the blade, then laid the knife down next to himself on the floor.

"When'd she live here?"

"I'm not sure."

"Then why'd you come here lookin' for her?"

"The police told me—"

Immediately, David knew he'd made a mistake.

"I thought you weren't no cop. Lyin' bastard."

"The police are trying to help find the little girl. That's all."

"Yeah. Right." He picked up the quart of Hamms and drained it. He set the one quart down and with seemless ease picked up a second one, uncapped it, and began making serious withdrawals from this one. "So who's this babysitter?"

"She lived in apartment six."

"Bullshit."

"What?"

"Nobody lives in apartment six."

"Maybe she moved recently."

"No way. That apartment's been vacant three years."

"What?"

"Three years minimum."

"Why is it vacant?"

"Had a fire in there. All burned out. Cheap bastard landlord's too cheap to fix it up again and he sure as hell can't rent it out the way it is. Not even in a neighborhood like this one."

"So nobody's been in there?"

A strange cackle came from the old man just as he lifted the quart to his lips again. Finished, he smacked his lips loudly. "I said it was vacant. But that don't necessarily mean that nobody's been in there."

"I don't follow you."

"You don't, huh? Now isn't that just too fuckin' bad?" The old man put forth, palm up, an amazingly steady hand. He snapped his fingers with all the arrogance he could summon. "You want talk, asshole, you're gonna pay for it."

"How much?"

"How much you got?"

"How much you want?"

"Asshole." Beat. "Twenty bucks."

"Ten."

"Fifteen."

David took his wallet out. He counted three crisp fives and handed them to the old man.

The old man lifted up the switchblade, set down the three fives, and then set the knife back down on the bills.

"So who goes in there?"

"This girl."

David sighed. This was a treacherous old sonofabitch, there was no doubt about it.

"You know her?" David asked.

"No. She only comes at night sometimes."

"What does she do?"

"Lets herself in."

"In apartment six?"

"Yeah."

"She has a key?"

"No."

"How does she get in?"

"That one you're gonna have to figure out for yourself."

"You have any idea what she does inside there?"

"No."

"You ever talk to her?"

Something shifted in the old man's expression. "I said I never talked to her."

Finally, David recognized what he saw in the old man's eyes now and heard in his voice.

"You're afraid of her, aren't you?"

The old man said nothing.

"Why would you be afraid of her?"

"I'll tell you somethin', mister. Just consider it part of the fifteen bucks." He took another swig from the brown Hamms quart. "You don't want to know that girl."

"Why not?"

"That's all I'm gonna say." He pointed to the door. His loose skin shimmied as he raised his arm. "Now you git."

"You don't know her name?"

"No."

"You don't know when she comes here?"

"No. Now git, just like I said."

"The landlord here?"

"Ain't no landlord. Just the real estate woman. Big tits. She comes once a week and checks things over."

"I want to go in there."

"Apartment six?"

"Yes."

The old man shook his head. "You're right, pardner. You ain't no cop. You're crazy is what you are. Crazy as shit."

"You going to try and stop me?"

"From going in there?"

"Yes."

The old man laughed. He sounded genuinely amused. "Hell, no. You go in there all you want."

David said nothing else. He crossed the floor, the aged oak floor creaking under his weight, turned the stereo back up to a decent level, then walked out of the apartment, closing the old man's door.

He walked back down the hall to No. 6. He tried the knob. Locked.

In TV shows, private detectives were forever using credit cards to tumble locked doors. Standing there in the murky light of the hallway, the stereo still twice as loud as it needed to be (the old man had turned it up, of course), the odor of cooking and garbage still turning his stomach, he tried the credit card.

What he got for his trouble, after a few moments, was an American Express card that was bent nearly in half. The door had not yielded at all. As he'd suspected, this trick only worked on doors with more modern lock systems.

He was more comfortable with what he tried next. The door was made of cheap pine and was probably half as old as the house itself.

It should not be too difficult . . .

The door's resilience shocked him. It also shocked the shoulder he'd just rammed into it. He was left leaning against the wall and rubbing a very sore spot just above his right bicep, where door and shoulder had made contact.

He was still rubbing his shoulder when he saw the old man appear in the hellish red light of his doorway. He grinned his toothless smile. Obviously he could see that David had tried ramming into the door. Obviously he could see that David had hurt himself trying to do so.

Above the din of the stereo, the old man said, "Only

way you're gonna get in there is kick the sumbitch. That's what I'd do."

Then he disappeared back inside his apartment, slamming the door.

David, continuing to work his shoulder, moved back from the wall and looked again at the door to No. 6. Though his ego was hurt—he wanted to feel at least as purposeful as "Magnum, P.I."—he supposed the old bastard was right. The card hadn't worked. Nor had his shoulder.

He figured out the best way to put his heel against the lock and then proceeded to push with his heel. The first time, it didn't work but he could feel—unlike his shoulder attempt—the door give at least a little bit.

The fifth time, it worked very well.

The heretofore impregnable door popped open with impressive implosion.

David went inside.

During his married years, he'd visited a friend's house that had been destroyed by fire. He recalled how all the wood was charred black, how to the touch it had felt bumpy, as if it were an animal covered with scales. He also recalled the odor. Fire always left a searing smell on the air, a smell that took years to go away. That smell was still in this room.

This apartment was laid out like the old man's, but instead of hellish red there was just the charred black and the big holes in the plaster walls from where the axes of firemen had pulled the chunks. The only illumination came from a streetlight that laid a dim pall over everything.

Some things had not been damaged. There was a couch, the cushions eaten up by fire. There was a daybed, the mattress stained from where the firemen's hoses had doused it. There was a bureau, the mirror on top shattered into a hundred fragments. It played back a very distorted image of David.

He found the phone in the corner. It was a model that David had used as a boy, the receiver resting on two slender prongs. Somebody had jerry-rigged it into the jack, which had remained undamaged in the fire. He lifted the cord trailing from its back and followed it through the darkness to a jack on a baseboard. He pulled the cord taut. It was still plugged in.

He went back to the phone itself and lifted the receiver. He got a dial tone. As many times happened when the phone company cut off service for overdue bills, the overdue party was left with a phone that allowed for calls out, but no calls in.

He replaced the receiver and began searching the apartment. He had no idea what he was looking for. In the third room, a kind of combination kitchenette and dining area, he found a box with canned goods and a stack of newspapers.

The papers interested him because they had been turned back to the want ads and certain ads had been circled. He carried the papers into the living room where he could use the spill light from the broken windows to examine the want ads more carefully.

A chill traversed his entire spine when he saw what section of ads had been noted—"Wanted, Babysitters."

What was even more disturbing were the dates of the papers. Though the old man said that the fire had gutted the apartment three years ago, these papers were mostly dated within the past two months. You could see where water from the hoses had splashed them.

He went through each paper, checking each circled ad carefully. In all, there were seventeen ads and each ran to type—credentials were required, pay was described as good, and phone numbers given.

All but the paper on the bottom, that is. Even touching that one told him instantly that there was something different about it. He took it even closer to the window for inspection.

It was a very old paper, the date given at the top read April 4, 1907. Though it was the local paper, much of the front page was devoted to national news of the time, particularly various examples of President Teddy Roosevelt's derring-do. Aside from a story about the mayor cutting the ribbon at a new bank (still in business today), there was only one other local piece. This one had been circled with the same ballpoint pen as the want ads.

The story was brief, describing the attempt by police to reclaim a two-year-old girl who had been kidnapped from a local orphanage by her mother. The mother, whom the county had judged insane, had lost the girl a year earlier. The woman was not named, nor were the orphanage or the girl. The language was so terse, it read like a police blotter.

He stuffed this paper, along with a few samples of the want ads, into his back pocket. He went back into the kitchenette area.

From a garbage sack next to a bulbous old Admiral refrigerator, he lifted the foil top of a TV dinner. He ran his finger over the foil. Tomato paste, he surmised, and at most two days old.

The girl, or somebody, had been here within the past forty-eight hours.

He opened the refrigerator. No interior light went on.

In the tiny freezer compartment, swollen with ice and badly in need of defrosting, he found two more Swanson TV dinners, one a beef patty and french fries, the other chicken with dressing.

He closed the door and went back into the living room. He picked up the phone and dialed Jody's number.

Her anxious hello told him one of the answers he'd wanted. Jenny had not been found.

"They're still looking," she explained, sounding miserable.

"How's Sam?"

"The pill worked. She's really out. Where are you?"

"It would take too long to explain right now, but I'd like you to do me a favor."

"All right."

"Who was the woman who gave Sam the babysitter's name?"

"Uh, Iris."

"Iris. Right. Would you call her back and ask her a question? It's pretty important."

"What question?"

"Ask her to think very carefully. Ask her if she ever called a number for this babysitter and got her. Or if the babysitter always called her."

"That's a really weird question, David. Aren't you even going to give me a hint?"

He looked around the big room. Down the hall the stereo had been turned up again. Hellish light would be spilling from the door. The toothless old man with his fading tattoos would be swigging from the quart bottle of Hamms. He was so pale his flesh seemed to glow.

"To tell you the truth, I'd like to get out of here. This place is starting to give me the creeps."

"What place?"

He laughed. "You're persistent, aren't you? I'm at the babysitter's apartment. Or at least a place she seems to come occasionally for some reason I don't quite understand."

"Why wouldn't she go to her apartment?"

"Because it was gutted three years ago in a fire."

"And she *lives* there?"

"I'm not sure if she lives here. But she visits here for some reason." He paused, thinking of the papers in his back pocket, and thinking of what the old man had said about her periodic visits. "Something brings her back here. At this point I don't know what."

"Have you talked with anybody who knows her?"

"Sort of. An old man who probably isn't the most reliable witness in the world."

"God," Jody said. "I just wonder what Jenny's got to do with all this."

"So do I."

"I just keep thinking of her, out there in the night somewhere and—"

He let her cry.

She went three minutes, maybe four, embarrassed sometimes, but sometimes just letting herself go. It was a process similar to bleeding yourself of poison.

At the end, she started to say, "I'm sorry," but he stopped her. "I thought we were friends."

"Well."

"Why would friends apologize to each other for crying?"

"Well."

"I know this sounds stupid, but I wish you'd relax."

This time, she laughed. "Actually, you're right. It does sound kind of stupid."

"Thanks."

Her voice softened. "God, David, I couldn't make it through this without you. I really appreciate—"

"Words you don't need to say. I'd like to think you'd do the same for me if I were in the same situation."

"You know I would."

"Good." He touched the papers in his back pocket. "Well, I'll see you in a while."

"Awhile? You're not coming back here now?" There was an edge of panic in her tone.

"No. There's a story I want to check out."

"A story?"

"Yes, one of the things I found up here was a newspaper from 1907. I'm not sure why, but I think it may have some bearing on the babysitter. I'm going over to the police station and ask if I can look through their old records."

"Do you think they'll let you?"

"Probably. Part of my town history devotes a whole section to the police. Winthrop has always been lucky. We've had good cops from day one. Anyway, they've been very cooperative and I've become friends with several of them. I'm sure, under these circumstances, that they'll let me check it out."

"Then you're coming back here?"

"Yes. Then I'm coming back there. In the meantime—"

"I know," she said ironically. "All I need to do is sit back and relax."

"Right," he said. "See you soon."

He had been so engrossed in his conversation that he

hadn't been aware that the apartment door had opened and that the old man had come in.

When David turned around and faced him, he nearly jumped.

"What the hell are you doing here?" David snapped.

The old man grinned. Even from here you could smell his breath. He carried his quart in his left hand. "My name's Rooney," the old man said. David backed away a foot or so.

"I might ask you the same thing," the old man said, grinning again. Then, "You got any more of them fives on you?"

"Maybe. Why?"

"Because I got something else you're gonna want."

"Such as what?"

"Huh-uh," the old man said with melodramatic craftiness. He put out his steady hand, palm up as usual. "First I get two more fives, and then I give you what I got."

Sighing, feeling as if he'd become an automatic teller machine for this pathetic old man, David pulled his wallet out and extracted a ten. He was out of fives.

He laid the crisp ten flat across the old man's palm and said, "Now, what are you going to give me?"

"This," the old man said. He reached in his own pocket and brought out a small card. "One time about five years ago there was this fairy who lived here. He said he was an artist, but he mostly kept himself alive by getting checks from his mother. Anyway, he made a habit of drawing everybody in this apartment house. One night he came over to my place, pretty hysterical. He said he'd been going to go over and see the girl who lived here, the babysitter you been askin' about, and how she didn't answer when he knocked. But her door was open so he went

105

in and called her name. Then he said he couldn't believe what he saw."

"What did he see?"

The old man handed him a folded piece of paper. It was heavy and rough, the stock artists use for pen and ink sketching and water colors.

David opened it up and looked at it. "This guy take drugs or what?"

"Smoked a little pot. That was about all, far as I can tell."

"He doesn't live here anymore?"

"Nope," the old man said. His grin was back. This time there was more than mischief in the grin. This time there was real malice. "Ain't you gonna ask me what happened to him?"

David sighed. "All right. What happened to him?"

"Fell down. Or so the story goes."

"Fell down?"

"Yeah. The basement stairs leadin' to the washer and dryer. Brain concussion, they said."

"Obviously, you don't believe that?"

"He died about twenty minutes after he gimme that sketch there." He paused, delighting in the effect his words would have. "He *told* me the babysitter was gonna kill him."

"You didn't tell the police all this?"

"You think the police'd listen to some old drunk bastard like me?" He shook his head. His flesh flapped, skin the white of fish bellies, faded tattoos like blood poisoning. "I just held on to that drawing. I figured someday it would be worth somethin'." He held up another quart. "I buy me generic beer, all this money you gimme tonight's gonna keep me goin' for three more weeks." He cackled.

"The babysitter."

"Yeah?" the old man said.

"She didn't know he'd made this sketch?"

"Apparently not."

"She never asked you any questions about the artist?"

"Nope. Far as she knew, I hated fairies just like everybody else."

"So you really think she killed him?"

"You bet your ass, pardner. You bet your ass." He tapped his head. "She ain't right. You look at her in the light sometime and you can tell that easy enough. She ain't right at all."

"And she doesn't show up here on any particular schedule?"

"None that I can see. Just sometimes late at night I hear her—or somebody—comin' up the stairs and comin' into this room."

For the first time, the old man shuddered. He looked as if he were getting caught up in his own tale. He turned, starting out of the room. Then he paused and looked back at David. "You take care of yourself, pardner." He waved the ten at David. "You're too valuable to lose."

With that he was gone, leaving David to take the sketch over to the spill light through the smashed window and examine it more carefully.

He wondered what it could possibly mean, this drawing of a woman's body topped with the head of a grasshopper?

Chapter Four

1

JENNY HAD CUT HERSELF PRETTY BADLY BY
falling on the gravel road and taking a chunk of flesh the
size of a silver dollar from her left knee. There was gravel
dust in the cut and the scabbing, and while she had
learned in Personal Hygiene that infection could cause
blood poisoning and that blood poisoning could ultimately cause a leg or an arm to be amputated if it wasn't
cleaned properly—still, she paid no attention.

She just kept walking down a narrow moonlit gravel
road, scrub pine and elm trees standing sentrylike on either side of the road, and the hot night alive with blood-
thirsty insects with prehistoric appetites for blood.

The insects didn't bother her, either, though. In fact,
nothing bothered her. There was a buzzing in her ears
that had at first given her a headache. But after a few

minutes she'd gotten used to it and right now that buzzing was her only reality.

She had no idea how long she had been walking. She had no idea where she was going. She had only the dimmest memory of being asleep in her bed in the rental house and the buzzing starting, and then she slipped out the back door while Grandma Jody and Mom were in the living room.

But she was not worried.

The buzzing would take care of her.

She wore her Nikes, she wore her Calvin Kleins, she wore her white tube socks with the red bands, she wore her white blouse with the hand-stitched rose on the right collar flap. She even wore her tiny pink barrette. She had put all these on when the buzzing started in earnest, dressing there in the dusk of her bedroom, trying to avoid making any sound so Grandma Jody and Mom wouldn't hear her.

She didn't know why, but for some reason it was important that neither Grandma Jody nor Mom find out where she was going.

But where *was* she going?

There were dogs in the night, and cows settling down under metal-roofed shelters, and pigs making sucking noises as they rolled around in the mud of their pens. There was the sound of cars on the two-lane highway and the sound of barn owls closer by. There was breeze trapped in trees and the sound of leaves sighing in the breeze.

She walked on.

In a half hour, she came to a roller coaster crest on the gravel road.

With instinctive certainty, she turned off the road and began a tortuous passage through thick bramble that began to cut at her with the ferocity of sharp little teeth. By now all this exertion had caused her to sweat a great deal. Her clothes were soaked, and vaguely (she felt very little) her eyes stung with perspiration.

Where am I going?

After a time, the bramble gave way to waist-high wild grass sloping down to a valley. She sneezed. She was a girl with many allergies, the one to milkweed being a particular nuisance. Moonlight shone on a patch of milkweed nearby.

She was halfway down the hill before she saw the cabin below. Actually, it was more of a shack than a cabin. Even from here she could see that it was a patchwork of rusted metal slabs and crumbling wood. Once, with her mother in the South, she'd seen many such shacks, her mother pointing out sadly that this was where black people lived.

She stumbled again, falling on her wounded knee, gashing it open even more. Fresh blood began trickling through the soft membrane of scabbing.

The starry night seemed so vast suddenly, the sky seemingly enormous, the woods next to the cabin as dark and immense as those in the fairy tales her mother used to read her, filled no doubt with mythic creatures meant to frighten eight-year-old girls.

When the ground leveled out, she smelled the stench from the cabin, the mingled odors of cooking and filth and—something she could not define, but something that gagged her.

For the first time, she paused in her single-minded journey. Did she really want to approach the cabin?

While one part of her mind pushed her forward, another part now began to hold her back.

Images of Mom and Grandma Jody formed in her mind.

She wanted to see them.

She wanted to *be* with them.

As she stood there, a hundred feet from the shack's door, doorsprings creaked and a woman appeared.

At first, in the shadows of the slab of wood used as a porch roof, it was impossible to see the woman clearly.

Jenny had the impression the woman was staring at her. Examining her.

Behind the cabin was a shallow creek. Frogs croaked in the silence now. Fish splashed.

The woman came out into the moonlight.

She was enormous, almost mannish, dressed in a ragged and faded house dress that only added to her massive size. Her iron gray hair was pulled back into a bun and her heavy arms were folded sternly across her chest. She was an Indian, her fleshy face unable to conceal her high cheekbones and the sharp jut of nose. She said, quite clearly above the frogs and the splashing fish and the distant dogs and the hooting barn owls, "She's been waiting for you."

Jenny knew better than to ask who *she* was. The little girl just stood in the small clearing, still divided between wanting to run to the shack and wanting to run back home.

When the woman took her hands from her chest, Jenny saw that in her right hand the woman held a small pistol. The woman said, "Don't be afraid."

It seemed a strange thing for somebody holding a gun to say.

Jenny, almost unaware of her own voice, said, "I think I'd better be getting back home."

"You know she won't let you do that."

"I'm scared," Jenny said.

The woman coughed up phlegm in her throat. She spat it deftly into the weeds. "I used to be scared of her, too, a long time ago. But not anymore."

"Why do you have a gun?"

The woman's fleshy face parted into a smile. Jenny thought she had never seen a woman more imposing or frightening. "It ain't for you, if that's what you're worried about." She nodded back to the shack. "It's just that she—she don't want uninvited guests. Sometimes we get hunters or fishermen cutting across here and I have to have this in case they want to hassle us or something." She spat again into the bushes, and only now did Jenny realize what she was spitting. Tobacco. The woman had a chaw firmly planted like a cancerous lump in her right cheek. "You know, most people around here believe my husband and me should be livin' on the reservation with all the other redskins." She managed to pack a lifetime's contempt into the word "redskins."

Jenny's head tilted backwards. She looked up the sloping hill. *Why did I come here? Can I get away?*

"She wants to see you, kid. It won't do no good to run. I'd just catch you, anyway." The woman paused. "Besides, she was the one who brought you here."

The woman took two steps forward and held out her hand again. This time it was the hand without the gun.

"We don't want to keep her waitin'," the woman said.

Once more, Jenny glanced back up the grassy, dusty hill. She contemplated bolting, taking her chances that the woman, bulky as she was, could not catch her.

Then the buzzing, which had abated ever since the appearance of the woman, began again.

Her entire body seemed to twitch with the buzzing.

The woman took several more steps forward.

The buzzing grew stronger inside Jenny.

The woman stretched her open hand out.

The buzzing—

Jenny accepted the woman's hand now without hesitation. It was a hard hand, unlike any female hand Jenny had ever touched before, iron strong and leathery and calloused. It closed on Jenny's small fingers like a vise.

They walked back toward the cabin, the ground giving way to a sandy area that proved somewhat difficult to walk in, Jenny twisting her ankle and falling on her injured knee. Roughly, the woman jerked Jenny to her feet and they continued walking. A lone weather-treated pole jutted up from behind the cabin. At the top of the pole were two heavy wires trailing off into the darkness.

The cabin's odors became more oppressive the closer they got. Made as it was of slabs—the wooden ones nailed together, the metal ones crudely welded together —the cabin had no windows, but through the screen door Jenny saw a candle glowing, revealing living conditions far more primitive than those of last summer's Blue Bird Camp. Two cots lay on the floor. Three folding chairs sat next to a table on which rested a large silver transistor radio. A few clothes, men's and women's alike, hung from a piece of rubber clothesline strung from one wall to the other.

But Jenny saw no *she.*

The cabin was empty.

The woman stepped under the overhang and pulled the

squawking door open for Jenny with a surprising formality. "Come on, kid, go inside."

Despite the buzzing noise that had now risen to an almost unendurable level—it was no longer a pacifying sound, the way it had been back in her bedroom or while she'd been walking out here—Jenny hesitated.

Seeing this, the woman took one of her big hands and put it on Jenny's shoulder. "Come on, kid." She sounded almost sad.

She gave Jenny a small but forceful shove.

Inside, Jenny stood on a tiny hooked rug and looked around. Up close, the place looked even worse, at best a shanty. One detail attracted her eye particularly. On the north wall was a painting of the Blessed Virgin, looking soft and beautiful in the faint glow of the candle. Except for one detail, that is. Someone had painted a lurid black mustache on the Virgin's upper lip.

The woman, seeing Jenny's displeasure, said, "You musta been raised Catholic, huh?"

Jenny said, "What's going to happen to me?"

The woman tapped her skull with the pistol's barrel. "You got the buzzing good and strong?"

"The buzzing in my head?"

"Yeah."

"Yes. It's very strong."

"Then you're gonna be fine. She'll see to that. Sometimes when the buzzing ain't strong . . ." The woman shook her head.

Jenny glanced around again. There was no sign of the woman she kept referring to. No *she*.

Jenny wondered if the Indian woman might not be insane. Perhaps the *she* was imaginary. When Jenny was smaller, she'd had all kinds of imaginary friends, particularly a Mr. Baubles who comforted her whenever she felt particularly sad. Perhaps for the Indian woman this *she* was a Mr. Baubles . . .

"I got to warn you about something," the woman said. "And understand, I'm sayin' this for your sake. All right?"

"All right," Jenny said hesitantly.

"Don't try and resist."

"What?"

"Some of them, they try to resist, even with the buzzing and all, and that's when it gets bad. Just give in right away and things will be easier."

"What things?"

In the flickering candlelight inside the reeking little shack, the Indian woman's eyes narrowed. "That's something you're gonna have to find out for yourself, kid."

Jenny decided to ask. "You keep talking about *she.*"

"Yeah?"

"But there isn't anybody else here."

The Indian woman laughed harshly. "So that's what's botherin' you! Because you can't see her?"

Jenny nodded.

The Indian woman laughed again. "Believe me, if I was you, I wouldn't be in too much of a hurry to see her." She spat an even brown stream of tobacco into a tin can resting on the floor. Then her eyes turned back to Jenny. "Nope, I wouldn't be in too much of a hurry at all."

She leaned over to the table. The remnants of a cooked chicken lay on a piece of foil. The woman's hand judo-chopped the black circle of flies covering the meat. After the flies were gone, she tore a piece of greasy flesh from the skeleton of the bird and brought it to her mouth.

Jenny wondered how you could eat with tobacco filling one side of your mouth.

Apparently, the woman had no problem.

Smacking her lips, wiping off some of the grease with the back of her hand, the woman said, "You go sit down over there."

"Where?"

"In that chair."

Jenny knew better than to argue. She went over and sat on the straight-backed chair. The legs wobbled.

The Indian woman walked past Jenny to where another small hooked rug lay. Kneeling down was an ordeal for the woman. She was like some massive animal incapable of easy movement.

Somehow, she got down on her knees. Her bones made cracking sounds and she gave out a sigh that was both pathetic and grotesque. Her face was slick with sweat. She lifted the hooked rug. Even in the shadowy light of the room, Jenny could see the outline of a door in the wooden floor of the shack.

The Indian woman pulled up the door and immediately the room was filled with an odor so sickeningly sweet, Jenny had to clamp her hand over her mouth to keep from vomiting.

It was then she heard the wailing sound for the first time. She did not know what else to compare it to except wailing, the way her dog Fritz had sounded when he'd gotten caught in barbed wire.

There was also the coldness, which seemed impossible to Jenny. A coldness that was at least forty degrees less than room temperature.

"You wanted to know where she was?" the Indian woman said. "Well, guess where?"

"My God," said Jenny.

"Now you get over here."

"My God," Jenny said again.

"You hear me, kid, you get over here."

"You're not going to make me go down in there, are you?"

The Indian woman looked both surprised and angry. "Where the hell else do you think I'd have you go? Chicago for a shopping spree?" She beckoned with the pistol. "Now you get over here."

"No," Jenny said. "No."

But now the buzzing became unbearable, and Jenny felt all her ability to fight leave her.

"Come on, kid. Come on."

Now the Indian woman's voice was faint, faint.

The coldness from the cellar began to dance around Jenny like wraiths enveloping her. At first she shuddered, and huge goose bumps covered her arms and legs.

But as she moved toward the cellar door—unable to stop herself—the coldness became what the buzzing had been earlier . . . comfortable, reassuring.

Jenny gave herself up, there at the last, to the buzzing.

To the coldness.

To the darkness of the cellar.

The Indian woman took her hand and helped her on to the first step of the ladder leading below.

Then there was just blackness and the wailing.

. . . the wailing.

2

"IRIS?"

"Yes."

"This is Jody again."

"Hi, Jody."

"Sorry to bother you so late."

"That's all right. We never go to bed till after Johnny Carson, anyway. What's up?"

"Jenny's missing."

Iris's voice tightened immediately. "What?"

"The police have been here already. They're looking through the neighborhood."

"My God." Beat. "How're you doing, Jody?"

"Trying to hang in there. That's about all I *can* do right now."

"You want Orn and me to come over and start looking for her, too?"

"No, Iris, that isn't why I was calling. I need to ask you a question again."

"Of course. Anything."

"That number you gave me."

"For the babysitter?"

"Right. Did you actually call it?"

"Yes. Why?" Then she stopped herself. "Wait a minute. Now that I think about it, I never did call that number."

"Why not?"

"Well, as soon as she was recommended to me, I heard from her."

"She called you then?"

"Yes."

Jody thought a moment. "Do you think it would be too late to call Agnes Thorp?"

"Nope. They're real pro wrestling fans, the Thorps are. She told me this afternoon that tonight's a special match. The Mambasi Mauler or somebody like that. I'm sure they're still up."

"Would you have her number handy?"

"Know it by heart, I call it so often." Iris gave her the number.

"Thanks, Iris."

"We'll be glad to come over and start looking."

"If we think we need the help, you'll be the first one I call."

"In the meantime, I'll be saying prayers."

"Thanks again, Iris."

She dialed Agnes Thorp's number immediately. A man answered. He sounded irritated that he'd been interrupted. In the background a huge crowd sound poured from a TV set. The Mambasi Mauler must have just pinned somebody. Jody wondered idly—giving her mind a needed momentary respite from Jenny's disappearance —if the Mauler was the good guy or the bad guy. The name didn't seem to delineate which.

"Agnes, please."

"Can I tell her who's calling?"

The man did not sound happy. She recalled him vividly. Larry Thorp. High school football hero who went into insurance and then into an unsuccessful local political career. Even as a boy, he'd never been happy, and Jody had never known why.

"Larry, this is your old classmate, Jody."

Most people would have greeted her with at least feigned surprise and pleasure. Not Larry. He merely grumped, "Oh, yeah, I heard you were back. Just a minute." Then he went away and shouted Agnes's name over the din of the TV.

When she came on, she said, "Hi, Jody." Her warmth made up for Larry's indifference.

"Hi, Agnes. Nice to speak to you again."

"What's it been? Nine years since our last reunion?"

"Something like that, Agnes. Something like that."

"Hopefully we'll get to see each other before you go."

"I hope so, too." She needed to get on with it. She said, "My granddaughter's missing."

"Oh no."

"I'd like to ask you a question about that babysitter you recommended to Iris."

"Oh, sure, her."

"Did you ever call her phone number?"

"What?"

"Did you contact her or did she contact you?"

Agnes hesitated. "Well . . ." She snapped her fingers. "No, I'll tell you how I heard about her. On the board at Schreiger's Market. There's one of those cork boards where everybody who's got something to sell puts their card. She had a card up there for babysitting. There was a phone number, but I didn't need it."

"Why not?"

"Believe it or not, she saw my girls at the playground one day and followed them home. Asked me if she could babysit for us sometime. She seemed nice and trustworthy, so I said sure."

"So you never called her number then?"

"No, I guess I didn't."

"And you used her only the one time?"

"Right. And not very long that time, either."

"Why not?"

"Larry got sick. We had some bad bratwurst at this cookout we went to down at the Eagles Club. Had to come home early."

"I see."

"You think the babysitter could have anything to do with Jenny?"

"We don't know. We're just trying to reconstruct the past couple days of Jenny's life."

"Is there anything we can do?"

"Were your kids the same?"

"Pardon me?"

"Did they seem any different after this babysitter was in your home?"

"No. Why?"

"Just curious is all."

"You're getting me spooked here, Jody."

Just then a second huge roar went up from the TV crowd. Larry roared right along with them.

Agnes said, "The Mauler just won."

"I'm happy for him."

"I'm sorry about Jenny. But I'm sure she'll turn up. You know how little kids—"

The conversation quickly turned into the same kind of pep talk Jody had received from the police. Grateful as she was for Agnes's good intentions, Jody thanked her and said good night as soon as possible.

Just as she hung up the phone, a creaking in the floor startled her, and her mind filled with an image of Jenny having come in the back door while she had been on the phone.

"Jenny!" she cried out.

Her voice in the stillness made her realize how alone

she was in this strange house. If it was not Jenny who was prowling the house, then who . . .

Feeling a fear that she hoped was irrational, she edged her way out of the kitchen and over to the hallway. The only light burning anywhere was in the living room which appeared, from first glance, to be just as she'd left it.

Still, the sense that something was wrong overtook her once more. From a wooden sideboard she picked up a small paring knife she'd used earlier in the day to slice tomatoes with. What a ridiculous weapon, she thought . . .

She moved into the hallway, listening carefully for any untoward sound. "Jenny!" she called again.

Nothing.

On tiptoes now, almost as if she were playing a child's game of hide-and-seek, she went down the shadowy hallway toward the far end of the house.

And then, blocking her way, the dark shape appeared.

The paring knife rose along with Jody's scream.

What startled her even more was that the dark shape also screamed.

"Mother! It's me!" Samantha shouted. "It's Sam!"

A ragged laugh of relief escaped Jody as she lowered the knife and fell into her daughter.

Hugging her, Sam glanced at the paring knife and said, "What were you going to do with that?"

"I—I thought I heard something. I just assumed you were asleep and I thought—"

She was incoherent and knew it. Her entire body still trembled from the odd encounter with Sam.

"Let's grab some soda and go into the living room." Then Sam put a hand on her mother's arm and said,

"You're not going to give me a speech if I smoke a cigarette, are you?"

Jody smiled. "Not this time."

"Good."

"I'll get the soda."

When they were seated—tinkling glasses of diet Pepsi in their hands—in the soft light of the living room, mother and daughter simply stared at each other.

Sam said, "They haven't found anything out yet?"

"No. But I wanted you to be sleeping. I—"

Sam shook her head. She looked groggy and hungover from the pills. "You know sleeping pills have never worked particularly well for me."

Jody sighed. "I guess that's true."

"Even when I was in de-tox that time. They'd give me sedatives and I'd wake up in an hour and a half. I always envied the people who slept through the night." She ran a hand through her hair. Even mussed, she was stylish and beautiful. Then a line of bitterness showed on her mouth. "I've been such a lousy mother. So goddamn selfish."

Jody knew there was no sense in trying to dissuade Sam from her self-loathing. Not now, anyway. It was a ritual she needed to perform. Jody said, "Honey, how do you think I feel?"

"What?"

"I've been a lousy mother, too. All those years drinking. Concentrating on my stupid little career—"

Sam lighted a cigarette. In the stillness, the paper match sounded like an explosion. She took the blue-white smoke deep into her lungs and held it there for a long time, as if she were smoking marijuana. She exhaled in a burst and then offered a lopsided grin. "How can anything so bad taste so good?"

"That's a terrible thing, isn't it? The way our pleasures are usually bad for us." She knew they were just small-talking. Each took turns watching the front door for signs of Jenny or the police.

Sam said, "When we find her, I'm going to stay here."

"In Winthrop?"

"Yes."

"How come?"

"I want to start all over. If I go back to New York—" She shook her head. She had another drag of her cigarette. The expression of bitterness returned to her face. "This is my fault."

"Honey, you know better than—"

"She probably got sick of it all. My behavior, I mean. That's why she got so crazy at Dr. Peary's this afternoon and that's why she ran away."

Jody wanted to say something wise about the burden of guilt and shame. But they were feelings she knew too well herself. And knew that there were no verbal antidotes for those feelings. You lived through them, accepted them sometimes, fought them other times, until one sober day you realized that remorse got you nowhere, that whatever time was left would be better spent in looking forward rather than backward.

Sam said, "I should have known the other night."

"Known what?"

"How upset she was."

"Why?"

Sam shrugged. "She told me about this dream."

"What was it?"

Sam smiled. "Stupid. You know how children's dreams can be. Something she probably picked up from a cartoon or something."

Jody said, preparing herself, "Was it a woman with the head of a grasshopper?"

Sam's head snapped up. "Did she tell you about it?" But it was obvious by her tone that she knew the answer would be no.

Jody shook her head. "There's something I need to tell you. About when I was a teenager."

Sam said, "You're starting to scare me, Mother."

"I don't mean to. But I think I'd better tell you. For some reason, I think it's got something to do with Jenny's disappearance."

"You mean you don't think she just ran away?"

"No, honey, I don't think so."

Sam stubbed out her cigarette. "Let me go to the bathroom first, okay? I'll be right back."

Jody nodded, remaining on the couch while Sam left the room. Mentally, she was back in 1953, the era of Jerry Lewis movies and Eddie Fisher records and Mom and Uncle Bob, both of whom had been killed in a car accident when Jody was a senior in high school—an accident that started her down the long road to alcoholism she later discovered in therapy. She thought of a particular night, the night she followed David Fairbain to Lorna Daily's house, a night that returned to her in dreams almost weekly. She saw the grotesque grasshopper-shaped head, and the peculiar tube extending from its jaws to the back of Lorna's neck. She saw the creature leaning forward as if supping, drinking . . . And then she thought of all the crazed things Lorna did afterward, particularly eating the dog, a story that seemed to live on long years after she'd been taken away by her parents . . .

And now Jody saw the sketch Jenny had drawn this

afternoon, with that same unmistakable shape for a head . . .

Sam was back. "You all right, mother?"

"Yes," Jody said, but her voice was ragged.

"So what did you want to tell me?" Sam said, sitting in the chair across the room.

Jody cleared her throat as Sam lighted a second cigarette. "Something happened to me when I was thirteen. Something I just assumed I could forget about until now. In fact, until today I wasn't sure that it really *had* happened to me. I thought that maybe my mind—"

There was silence.

Sam exhaled smoke.

Jody tensed her hands into small fists. She had never told anyone, anyone, of what she'd seen that night. She was not certain why—pride probably, afraid she'd be looked at as foolish or worse. It was just not the kind of story you told . . .

"The summer I was thirteen," Jody began.

It was not an easy story to tell. Not an easy story at all.

3

YOU WERE ALWAYS DOING BUSINESS. YOU could have your mouth stuffed full with beef tenderloin (he liked his pretty bloody) or setting your little white ball on to the tee or peeing at a urinal . . . and you were always doing business. You had to see who was next to you and think about what kind of car he was driving these days, and figure out the best way to pitch him on a Caddy. Because the old days were over, the days of Glen

Stover's youth when everybody who was anybody in Winthrop had just automatically wanted a Caddy. They just weren't the status symbols they'd once been, and it wasn't just the heat they'd been taking since the fifties and the emergence of Lincolns; no, now it was a variety of foreign jobs as well, particularly the frigging Benz. These days the Mercedes was the status symbol—just take a quick glance at the parking lot—and you found yourself vaguely apologetic and even a little defensive when you pitched somebody on Caddies. You didn't want to come right out and use the WWII logic—all the American boys the Krauts had killed, and how we'd built up their economy just so they, along with the Japs, could return the favor by economically slashing our throat—so you always talked about how Detroit, especially General Motors, and especially the Cadillac division, had been putting out one mighty fine automobile the past couple of years. No more of this stuff where the doorknobs fall off sometimes, or where the chassis squeaks develop in the first couple hundred miles or so, or where the engine stalls at sixty or any of those other problems they were having a few years back. No, sir. No way. Not now. The Caddy was once more the car it used to be, an *American* car, not some frigging kraut Benz. An *American* car.

Thus far tonight he had hit on every major category (he tended to think of people that way; not so much as individuals but rather as representatives of various professions). He had hit on lawyers (lawyers being know-it-alls, unfortunately, and notoriously tough sells), doctors (their wealth vastly overestimated due to their legendary inability to invest their money properly and consequently giving up about seventy percent of their income to an uncle named Sam), CEOs (their problem being that while they might individually *prefer* a Caddy, they couldn't afford to be perceived as driving something lesser than most of their peers), and the unemployed wealthy who spent their days playing golf and looking for ways to safely make their inheritance work for them. The unemployed wealthy were actually his best prospects because they had plenty of time to hang around the showroom and let Glen Stover give them the full benefits of his sales technique.

Thus far tonight, he'd lined up six appointments stretching over the next three weeks: two lawyers, a doctor, and three CEOs. Of the six, only two had previously owned Caddies, which was a curse if those Caddys had been manufactured between 1978 and 1983 (the worst product the division had ever put out), but a blessing if their Caddies had come from any other year, because dollar for dollar and feature for feature, Glen Stover was prepared to *prove* that the Caddy, screw the Krauts, was the best value on the market.

He had had six drinks. Marietta had asked him to limit himself to three. For her sake, for his sake, for the sake of the dealership, and not least for the reputation of her family, which had, after all, been among the club's founders. And this being the beginning of the one hundredth anniversary . . .

He was drunk and he was bored and he hated tuxedos. He sat at a small table near the edge of the dance floor and deeply resented the fact that his life was going by him so quickly. Sometimes it seemed to him as if he were witnessing a stranger's life, as if he had no control whatsoever over his days and nights. It would be the end in twenty or thirty years and he would not have understood a moment of it, not really. He would have been this *thing* trapped inside a body known as Glen Stover. A thing that had never known the happiness or the gentleness or the peace it had so long and uselessly sought . . .

"Are you all right, dear?"

He looked at her without recognition. Booze and inner turmoil had blinded him, literally.

She patted his hand, leaning in over the candle flickering inside the red glass of the tablelight. "Are you all right?"

His wife.

Talking to him.

Asking if he was all right.

"Yes," he said. "Yes."

Still her face, her quite beautiful face, remained hovering there in the flattering glow of the candle, and she smiled at him and he remembered the first date they'd had, how nervous she'd made him even though he was far more experienced than she. And how for a time she'd changed him and the happiness and the gentleness and the peace he'd sought had been so near . . . so near . . .

"I'm going for a walk," he said, standing up abruptly.

"Like me to go with?"

He hated that expression. It irritated him beyond reason. "Go with." What was wrong with "Go with you?" Cutesy. God, he hated cutesy.

"Not unless you want to see the inside of a men's room."

There. Now her kind and concerned words about his well-being had been dashed, and their relationship was back on more familiar turf.

He wobbled away from the table, pitching himself into the crowd of people who looked too young, too pretty, too handsome, too strong, too rich, too powerful. He wanted to slap them. He wanted to slap them because they reminded him of his brother . . .

The club was gorgeous. Even in his condition, he could appreciate that fact. Oak and mahogany and green carpet so thick it was like walking through pastureland. And paintings. God. Beautiful Grant Woods and Marvin Cones celebrating the Midwest as it damned well should be (even if it wasn't). He passed from one fantastic room to another, where young women with flesh he could scarcely keep his hands from sat throwing their lovely heads back in practiced laughter, and where men exuded a musky scent of lust and power, the two things often being one and the same.

He was no longer young, Glen Stover. And something like a double chin had started beneath the good Stover bones of his face. And his waistline, if not a pot, was anything but flat. And when he smiled at the young ladies now, they smiled back with a certain pity, as if he had been caught doing something foolish.

There were rooms with giant fireplaces and rooms with billiards, the clack of balls caught up in the soughing wind through the huge mullioned windows, and rooms with dry bars, and rooms with formal dining arrangements.

The Cadillac dealer acted a certain way. Or should. And so he found within himself sobriety, or something resembling it, and so for his betters there was the ingratiating and slightly toadying smile, and a formal nod to the ladies and a remark on the dazzle of their gowns or their hair.

He wandered through all three floors of the club, the

vast stone innards of this domain where six generations of Stovers had dominated the politics within these walls.

Then he came, in a corner of the first floor west of the swimming pool, to the portrait of his brother Evan. Standing there, chlorine smells sobering him even faster, he stared at the portrait of the handsome twenty-five year old who had been killed while serving as a Marine pilot in Vietnam.

When he was certain that no one was around, he leaned back enough to do it right, and he spat directly on the painting of his dead brother's face.

Bastard.

Had he lived, Evan would have been two years older than Glen. He also, Glen was certain, would not have been content to inherit what remained of the family fortune and run the dwindling Cadillac franchise.

No, dear-bright-pretty-winning Evan would have parlayed the remnants of the family jewels into a fortune of significant count. He would have been president of the club, not merely a member, and most likely run for a house seat as a Republican from the 4th district, much as their Uncle Benjamin, now a United States senator, once had. His wife would have been twice as beautiful as Marietta (and with good ankles), his children would have been setting records both as scholars and athletes, and his company would have been sought by those powerful men who found Glen to be a lightweight.

He watched the spittle roll down his brother's face and began recalling how dinner always went when they were boys. And what did you do today, Evan? Oh, isn't that marvelous, dear; did you hear what Evan did today? Evan Evan Evan.

Never had there been room in his parents' hearts for

Glen, and now that he was grown he could understand why. He was passable. That was the proper word for him. Passable. Passable grades, passable looks, passable ambitions, passable accomplishments. But not the sort of boy a person, at least not a Stover, boasted about or doted on.

Passable.

He could not even join the Army for Vietnam. At age sixteen he had injured his knee in a baseball game, and ever since the knee had locked on him at odd times.

He could not even lay down his life for the greater glory of the Stovers . . .

He glared up at the portrait once again. Visiting his parents these days, you would have thought Evan was still alive. Evan this, Evan that.

Still not a word for Glen . . .

"Maybe you'd better sit down, Glen. Really." She always said "really" in that soft, almost whispered way when she was serious.

He pulled away from her grasp. How the hell had she found him anyway?

"I said I wanted to go for a walk," he said. "I meant alone."

"No room for your wife?"

He started to say no, but decided that would only be useless cruelty. "You see what I did."

Her eyes found the silver spittle on Evan's face. "Yes."

"Aren't you going to tell me I should be ashamed of myself?"

"You know you should be ashamed of yourself. I don't have to tell you that."

"I hated him."

"I know."

"Always so goddamn perfect."

"That's how it appeared, anyway."

"Meaning what, exactly?"

"Meaning that he wasn't perfect, Glen. Nobody is."

"Try telling that to my parents."

He smiled and slid his arm around her waist. Hers was the flesh of a forty-year-old woman. Much as he was sentimental about her at the moment, hers was not the kind of flesh he needed just now.

He thought again, for the hundredth time this evening, of the babysitter—Nikki—and of the exact moment when his hand had brushed her breast. Had he detected the slightest approval in her glance? Could she possibly have been interested in a man his age?

"Why don't we go back in now?" she said. Now it was her turn to smile. "Maybe you can sell a few cars."

"I'm too drunk to sell cars."

"You sound a lot better than you did twenty minutes ago."

"Maybe I'll go for a drive."

"I thought you were drunk."

He grinned at her. "Not too drunk to drive."

"That isn't funny."

He shook his head. "I'm not drunk. Here. Look."

He proceeded to perform, there on the carpeting before the spittle-dripping portrait of his brother, there before the genuine George III mahogany and satinwood sideboard that sat beneath the portrait—he proceeded to perform a reasonable facsimile of the test a police officer would put him through to judge his sobriety.

"Pretty good, huh?" he said, touching his fingertip to his nose and walking a rigidly straight line.

"A lot better than I would have thought," she said behind him.

He stopped, turned around. "Now may I go for a ride?"

"I'm really not up for a ride."

"I didn't mean you, anyway."

"Thanks."

"I need to be alone. I'm sorry if that hurts your feelings, but it's the truth."

She said, "It's a woman, isn't it?"

"God."

"Is there somebody new at the dealership? A secretary I haven't met? That Cuban receptionist back for the second time through."

"Some marriage we have."

"Then you weren't unfaithful all those times."

"People change, you know."

"Some do. Sometimes."

"It's just a ride. Really." He made sure to say "really" the way she always did. He kissed the side of her mouth. The longer they were together, the more he found himself addressing her as he would a combination wife-mother-jailer. A certain whine. A certain pleading. He had noticed this in other men, too, how they ended their days as children, with their wives playing the role of mothers.

"I don't know why I put up with it," she said. She was tall enough, on tiptoes, to stand up and daub a clean white handkerchief on the portrait. She picked up the spittle and then dropped the handkerchief into an ashtray.

Whether she knew it or not, he noted, she had just picked up after him. As a mother would.

"I'll be back in an hour or so. Honest."

"I'd appreciate it if you'd keep your word, Glen. I'd

hate to have to bum a ride with somebody. That would be pretty shabby for both of us."

"An hour."

He went to kiss her again. She put a firm hand against his chest, stopping him.

"You don't want to kiss me," she told him.

He didn't bother to disagree.

He had a convertible tonight. A white one. The air was fresh and the moon seemed almost spectral.

At a downtown stoplight two punks in a modified Chevrolet pulled up next to him. One of them started to say something, but then, curiously, stopped.

Glen Stover had managed to put in his expression exactly what he was feeling. That receding hairline or no, that spreading middle or no, he would take this dirtball's head off, if the dirtball so much as breathed a single syllable in Glen's direction.

A single syllable.

When the light changed, the Chevrolet peeled out and the punks naturally shouted something back at him, something lost in the squeal of rubber and roar of engine.

But he knew who had won the confrontation, and so did they.

Damn, maybe that little babysitter was going to be happy about his surprise visit after all.

4

SHE HAD A CIGARETTE, A CHESTERFIELD King, one nabbed from a stout man in a handsome red silk dinner jacket. The last time she had had a cigarette was on the night her father had died. She had never smoked before in her life. But somehow it seemed the right thing to do, to ask her brother for a smoke.

And now, sitting at the bar, the din of the band and the drunken conversations furious as war, it was for the second time in her life the right thing to do.

Tonight, she even managed to inhale without coughing, taking the blue smoke deep within her lungs, and blowing it back out in an almost pretty stream.

She sat there with her drink (Scotch on the rocks) and her cigarette and nobody bothered her. She wasn't the type. Perhaps, she thought, with a curious kind of self-mischief; perhaps it's my ankles. And then she had to smile. How long she'd hated her ankles; how many years.

She realized quite abruptly that she was drunk. She was now guilty of two things she'd done only twice in her life—smoking and drinking to excess.

She began, despite herself, to watch couples on the floor, dancing slow now that the band was doing saxophone ballads, couples silhouetted romantically in the soft white light of the bandstand.

Couples . . .

She wondered where he was going tonight. A quickie, no doubt. She wondered with whom. She had not been jealous of him in years, and she surprised herself with the ferocity of her feeling.

But quickly as it had come, it was gone, that feeling, and she was left at the bar noticing for the first time how the stray gaze would travel to her and then quickly look away.

They knew, those watching her, knew and felt sorry for her. And that being the last thing she wanted, she eased herself from the barstool, stubbing out her cigarette as she did so, and went off with a certain urgency in the direction of the phone.

She had decided to call home and see how the babysitter, Nikki, was doing with the girls. She wasn't sure why, but suddenly she sensed something wrong with her daughters. Perhaps it was nothing more than the effects of the alcohol . . .

5

JENNY HAD NO IDEA HOW LONG SHE HAD been in the basement. When the Indian woman had pushed her down there, all Jenny had been able to see was darkness. All she had been able to feel was the grave-like coldness of the damp clay walls.

After a time, Jenny had come to realize that she was not alone.

In the far corner of the basement, something inhaled and exhaled deeply every half minute or so, the breathing labored, the way someone on a respirator breathed.

Twice Jenny had said, "Would you please tell me who you are?"

There had been no direct answer, but the buzzing grew louder in her ears.

Just now, the creature in the corner moved. There was a rustling of fabric and a sound of something solid striking the floor. Jenny peered through the blackness, trying to see. The breathing sounds became heavier.

"Please tell me who you are," Jenny pleaded again. "Please."

Without warning, hands were on her, hands she at first mistook for human as they clamped on her shoulders and pulled her forward.

But when her own hand came in contact with the creature's leathery flesh, Jenny realized with disgust and panic that the flesh was not human at all.

Jenny screamed.

It did no good.

The hands dragged her forward.

Chapter Five

1

THERE WAS A FAMILY JOKE ABOUT THREE-year-old Annie Stover. The joke was about her bladder and her frequent nighttime trips to the bathroom. "Six and counting," her mother always laughed. Then six-year-old Hedley would laugh, and then Daddy would laugh, too.

Suddenly, confined by the swirl of sheets pulling at her like a whirlpool, Annie was awake. Rubbing her eyes and trying to figure out what had awakened her. Because, for once, she didn't need to pee.

Moonlight through the French windows lent everything in her room the kind of deep shadows Annie associated with the scary movies Hedley always liked to watch on HBO. Annie looked around the room, hoping it would soon appear more familiar and reassuring.

Then she heard the sound again and knew at once it was the same sound that had awakened her.

She wondered what the sound was. She knew what it sounded like . . . like a huge snake hissing without pause.

The room a bit less ominous now, Annie set one foot that tingled with sleep to the floor. She smacked her lips, realizing how thirsty she was. She needed a glass of water. She set her second foot to the floor and stood there in the moonlight, letting the silver wash spread a curious warmth through her pink cotton pajamas.

A minute later she eased open her door and peered out into the hallway. Even with the best of babysitters, she never felt comfortable when Mom and Dad were gone. But maybe they were home now. Maybe it was one of the impossible-to-imagine times, such as 3:00 or 4:00 A.M., and maybe Mom and Dad were asleep in their bed right down the hall.

But somehow she thought not.

The silence struck her as odd, and so did the fact that no lights burned downstairs.

Wouldn't the babysitter be reading or eating a sandwich or something?

Annie ventured out into the hallway. Sweat began to paste her pajama top to her back. Now she did have to go to the bathroom.

She walked down the hall to the master bedroom, her bare feet feeling at intervals the smooth luxury of real Persian rugs. She opened the door wide. Shadows played across the white expanse of the bed. The empty bed.

Mom and Dad weren't home.

Her tiny hand still on the big silver doorknob, she reshut the door and went back down the hall to the bathroom.

The toilet seat, because of the air-conditioning, was cold on her bottom. She had a quick, good pee and felt much better afterwards.

While she was washing her hands, and reaching up for a towel, she heard the sound again.

The hissing.

She ran to the hallway, hands dripping soap, and listened.

Now it sounded like breathing, the heavy, almost painful way Dad had sounded when his bronchial condition acted up last winter.

But it couldn't have been Daddy breathing. Daddy wasn't here.

Ducking back into the bathroom, she dried off her hands, reached up on tiptoe to turn off the light, and then went back out to the hallway.

Instinctively, she began moving toward Hedley's room. Even if the sound wasn't coming from Hedley's bed, Annie planned to tell her older sister just how weird everything was all of a sudden—the lights off downstairs; the hissing noise up here—so Hedley could reassure her that everything was going to be all right.

Hedley's door was closed.

Annie moved up to it, put both hands on the knob, and with her whole body pushed in.

As soon as she'd done so, she knew exactly where the sound was coming from.

Here.

Hedley's bed was around the corner of the room, away from the windows and sunlight that Hedley hated early in the morning. Consequently, Annie could not see her bed from here. But she certainly could hear the hissing.

Without knowing why, Annie was afraid to go any farther into the room.

Afraid of her own sister? God!

From here she could see the big wooden toy box with the dolls and scooters and teddy bears arrayed in a very neat line along the front of the box. Mom always called Hedley "persnickety," meaning, as close as Annie could figure out, that she got real mad if anything got out of place. She sure could get mad at Annie, anyway, when Annie messed up something in Hedley's room.

"Hedley."

No answer.

"Hedley."

No answer.

Annie could never remember hearing the house so quiet. Now, as if somebody had been caught doing something they weren't supposed to, now even the hissing stopped.

There wasn't even the blowing noise of the air conditioner.

"Hedley. It's me. Annie. Are you over there?"

Nothing.

"Hedley."

Annie took two steps toward the sharp angle of corner silhouetted in front of her. If she could get close enough to the corner and just sort of peer around it, then maybe she wouldn't have to go all the way over to Hedley's bed. She had convinced herself that the trouble was simple enough: Hedley was alseep and not able to hear Annie. But when Annie got to the edge of the corner and called her name, Hedley would wake up for sure.

Annie flattened herself against the wall, the way she'd seen private detectives do on those shows that Daddy always liked, and inched her way up to the end of the wall so she could peek around. The only other time her heart had ever beat this quickly was when Hedley had accidentally locked her in the basement and Annie, after an hour of yelling, had become convinced that she would never be found, and that at night monsters of various types would appear from the shadows and eat her.

Now, it was time.

She stood there, and all she had to do was just kind of turn her face to the left and take a quick glance back—and then she'd be able to see that sleepyhead Hedley was in bed, and probably snoring, and that was why she hadn't answered Annie.

Annie turned and looked and started screaming immediately.

She also began running as fast as she could out of Hedley's room, tripping once over the hooked rug by the walk-in closet and banging her knee hurtfully, but not slowing down much at all.

She couldn't stop screaming.

Couldn't.

She ran down the long, curving staircase into the deep ocean of blackness below. When she reached the massive front door, she continued screaming, but now she was also sobbing, because now she had some sense of what had happened to her sister Hedley in her bedroom upstairs.

Annie got the door open and almost hurled herself out into the night.

She went straight for the huge oak that sat on the crest of the hill upon which their house had been built. She knelt by the oak and clung to it with outstretched hands, as if it were all the mommies and daddies in the world, because after what she had seen, it would take that many mommies and daddies to make her terrifying thoughts go away.

She had no idea where she could go next.

All she knew for sure was that nobody was ever going to get her to go back into that house.

Ever.

2

GLEN STOVER HAD BEEN STOPPED ONCE FOR drunk driving and he had been damned mad about it, pointing out to the arresting officer (a kid with freckles and braces!) that his name was Glen Stover, that Stover's *père* built not only the hospital, but the football stadium and the Vietnam memorial in the center of City Park, and the fastest way to get in trouble in this town was to fuck with anybody who possessed, by blood or ceremony, the name Stover.

Seemingly untroubled, the kid (Stover wondered if he even had to shave yet) wiped sweat off his palms, leaned into the Caddy, jerked the keys from the steering post, and escorted Glen Stover first to the squad car and then to the county jail.

All kinds of hell was raised right after dawn, but until dawn Glen Stover had resided in the drunk tank with two of the most brutish men he'd ever seen, day laborer buddies who each had HATE tattooed on their knuckles, and who picked on Stover unmercifully all night. The funny thing was, though, the Chief did drop the charges, but he didn't offer any apology for what the kid had done. About the only thing he did offer was a warning, sounding like a frigging auto safety commercial on TV. "Glen," he said, "just about the most useless way you or your kids can die is to have some fucking drunk run into you." He'd even waggled a finger. "Now the next g.d. time one of my officers catches you drunk behind the wheel, I'm really going to come down on you. You understand?"

Except for his father, nobody had ever talked this way to Glen Stover before. He found the man's temper and sincerity fascinating in a weird way. Damn, but that guy had been mad.

Glen recalled all this as he drove approximately ten miles below the speed limit on the way back to his house. He still had vague intentions of seeing if the babysitter might be induced to join him in a little harmless sex, though by now his ardor had cooled, and his memory of spitting on the portrait of his brother had come to sicken him. There were times in his life when he saw exactly what a spoiled shit he was, and then for a time he would be better. Even drunk, he was going through one of those periods of remorse now, and thinking what a fine good woman he'd married, and what a terrible bastard he'd been to her.

He didn't notice the car following him closely. Not for the first five miles anyway. He sat in an exaggeratedly straight way behind the wheel, his hands locked like vises onto the sculptured blue steering wheel. He kept staring at the speedometer. Although he knew that one sure way to spot a drunk was to look for any cars that were just putting along—though he knew this, he figured overcompensating would help. He didn't know what else to do.

And suddenly he felt lost and alone, a man who now wanted nothing more than his own bed, where he could sleep off the booze and the venom.

The car forcing him off the road and into the curb was the damnedest thing he'd ever seen. It came swooping up, started to pass him, and then crowded right into a concrete gutter running along the west phalanx of Brady's Golf Course.

Not until she came up to the Caddy, opened the door and edged him into the passenger's seat, did he recognize his wife Marietta.

"What the hell are you doing?"

"Now, Glen, what do you think? I borrowed Trish James's car and came after you. She said she could catch a ride." She sounded very calm and very sensible as she pulled the Caddy away from the curb, leaving the James's car locked for the night. "You may not remember, but Chief Carella called me the morning we had to come down and get you. He told me what would happen to you next time." She looked over at him, the moonlight and the dashboard light painting the lovely bones of her face with an odd burnished color. She was stunning, and in that moment he knew that he still loved her, however many times he'd strayed, however many times he'd been such a shit.

He said, "I know what you say about people who make pledges when they're drunk."

She glanced over at him and smiled. God, did she have a great smile. "Good, dear. I'm *glad* you remember."

"But I want to make one."

"A pledge?"

"Yeah."

"Well, I suppose, you being bigger than me, I really couldn't stop you."

"Good."

"But that doesn't mean I'll listen."

"Thanks."

"Or take you seriously even if I do listen."

"Great."

"But that shouldn't stop you. I mean, we're just riding along, you may as well make a pledge. There really isn't anything else to do."

She was teasing him the way she used to when they'd first started going out, and God he'd loved it then. Nothing in his life had ever made him feel as important as her teasing. Somehow her wry words were proof that she loved him, better than ten thousand I-love-yous. He'd loved her teasing then and he loved it now.

"I've been a shit."

"Oh, I wondered if it wasn't going to be that one."

"What?"

"The I've-been-such-a-shit pledge."

He laughed. "Damn you."

"Now there's a friendly thing to say."

"I just meant—"

"That you've been," she said, "a terrible husband, a terrible father, and a terrible friend, and why in God's name do you still love me, Marietta? Isn't that how that one goes?"

He was laughing too hard to answer.

"But didn't you leave out something? Isn't there a sentence or two about how all this is going to change, just as soon as you wake up in the morning? Don't I remember something like that?"

"You know I love you."

"I know."

"And you know I really am sorry."

"I know."

"And I really don't know why you put up with me."

"I know you don't."

"And I really wish there were some way I could make up for all the things I've done."

"Saying you love me helps."

"Really?"

"Really, Stover. I don't know why myself, but I've never gotten tired of hearing you say it. As mad as I've been, as hurt as I've been, as disappointed as I've been, I guess I've always melted at least a little when you said it."

"I really am going to change."

"I know you want to."

"I'm going to change for you."

"You should change for yourself. I think that's the only way those things work."

"Then I'll change for myself and the girls."

"I guess they'd be worth changing for, the girls," she said, and soft tears came into her eyes and voice. She put out her hand and he took it. Gently.

He kissed her hand.

"You haven't done that in a long time."

"It's nice to know I'm not *completely* predictable."

She looked at him and smiled. "Yes, I suppose it is."

They were taking the long blacktop curve that led to their estate, a quarter mile of white pine and birch trees, the pine a spectral color now in the moonlight, the night air (he'd cracked his window some time ago) rich with heat and flowers.

"I love you," he said again.

He said this just as Annie appeared in the headlights, her eyes wild, her nose running, and blood soaking one of her knees. Even above the thrum of the motor and the steady *whooosh* of the air conditioner, the Stovers could hear her screaming.

Stover was out of the car before Marietta braked to a complete stop. The taillights were blood red in the late night darkness.

3

"IN 1907 AN INDIAN WOMAN WAS FORCED by the local authorities to give up her baby for adoption."

"Why?"

"Well, first of all, the woman had a drinking problem that was so bad she was even ostracized from the reservation. She was forced to live up in the hills east of here. It was believed—or rumored anyway—that the woman was heavily involved with the Indian occult world, putting curses on people and trying to summon up demons. That was the second strike against her, and ultimately why the authorities took her daughter from her."

"Even if she was crazy," Jody said. "It's still sad to think of her having her daughter taken."

"It sure is," Sam said. She sat next to her mother on the couch. Across from them, seated anxiously on the edge of a recliner, David Fairbain eagerly shared with them everything he'd discovered at both the library and in the files of the local police.

"So after the authorities took the little girl, the Indian

woman went to the orphanage and tried to get the girl back?" Jody asked.

David nodded. "Tried. They caught her with a two-year-old in a large carpetbag the woman, Noawa, was carrying."

"She came close then," Sam said.

"Very close," David said. "And that's probably why the authorities were so harsh with her."

"What did they do?"

"Put her in a mental home. They had a nicer name for the place, of course—the police department files refer to it as a rest home."

"How long was she in there?" Jody asked.

"Fourteen years."

"My God."

"Did she ever see her daughter again?"

David shook his head. "This is the really sad part. Her daughter died of pneumonia in the orphanage when she was twelve years old."

"Did they tell the mother?"

"Not until after she was released from the home."

"What did she do then?"

David again shook his head. "That's just it. Nobody knows for sure. Some people on the reservation who knew Noawa felt that she probably went west to Wyoming, where she had relatives. But others insisted that she stayed around here, back up in the hills, and took up where she left off with her interest in the occult." He paused. "It was a few months after her release that things started happening to young girls."

"What sort of things?" Sam asked. Obviously, she had started worrying about Jenny again. She was biting her nails with ferocity. Every few moments, her left hand would twitch.

David looked at Jody. "You know what happened to Lorna Daily?"

Jody nodded.

"Things like that." He turned to Sam. "A young girl would seem perfectly normal one moment, then the next she would be attacking people. Really violently. The police as long ago as 1921 began to see a pattern in all this, so they've kept all the information in a single file. When you see that maybe as many as five girls have been affected by this—lost their minds literally—you see how ominous it is."

"And you think this has happened to Jenny?" Sam was up on her feet. She was also practically shouting.

Jody got up and took her daughter in her arms. "Honey, listen, please. Jenny just probably wandered off. That's all."

David said, "Sam, why don't you let me call your doctor and see if giving you another sleeping pill would be all right."

Sam began crying. "But I want to know where Jenny is." She sounded frenzied. "I want to know where my little girl is."

"Come on, honey, come on now," Jody said. She nodded to David. He went into the kitchen to use the phone.

After a few minutes, Sam lay down on her mussed bed. Jody went over and closed the drapes. The moonlight seemed unnaturally bright tonight. Sam lay with her robe off, just in white panties and a bra. She made a sound not unlike a moan.

"Mom, you really think she's going to be all right?"

"Yes, honey, I really do."

"You don't think there's any connection between what David found out and—"

"Honey, David didn't find out anything except about a few coincidental occurrences, and we don't even know for sure those actually took place. Even David said that most of the things said about Noawa were rumors."

"But her interest in the occult—"

Jody leaned forward and wiped a thin layer of perspiration from Sam's head. "Millions of people are interested in the occult. And in a town this size, I doubt it's all that uncommon for five girls to have mental problems from 1921 till now."

"You really mean that?"

"Sure, I do, honey." Jody felt guilty about lying so glibly, but for now she had but one task. To get her daughter to sleep.

A minute later, David arrived with a small glass of water and two yellow tablets. "The doctor said Sam could take *both* of these as a matter of fact."

"Thanks, David," Jody said, taking the water and pills and handing them to Sam.

When Sam was finished with the water, she lay back, and Jody began stroking her forehead again. Hundreds of memories numbed Jody—Sam at First Communion, Sam winning the fourth grade spell-down, Sam's first ninth-grade dance and the blue gardenia corsage. Jody wished there were some way to tell her troubled child just how much she really loved her, but any attempt to express it in words was doomed to a few cliches and nothing more.

Sam must have wanted badly to sleep, because she gave herself over to the pills very quickly. Within ten minutes, small soft snores came from between her lips, and a well-shaped arm dangled from the bed.

Jody stood by the bed, glad that David had taken the liberty of putting his arm around her shoulder. Jody broke away to kiss Sam good night.

Back in the living room, Jody said, "I wanted you to be truthful with Sam. Now I don't know if that was a good idea."

"She'd have to know eventually."

Jody eyed him curiously. "Know what?"

David sighed. "Jody, you know damn well what. And you also know damn well what's going on around here. You remember Lorna Daily."

The name chilled Jody. She thought again of the beautiful young girl who had savagely attacked her parents, and then only a few days later attacked and eaten a neighborhood dog. "Yes," she said. "I remember Lorna."

"The police have her on their records."

"Lorna?"

"Yes."

"And you really think Jenny—?"

"I can't be sure, but the pattern is sure the same. A babysitter in the previous forty-eight hours, a brief disappearance, and then a return home where they begin to exhibit really psychotic behavior."

"But we don't know that any of that will happen."

"No, we don't. Not for sure."

"But you think it will?"

"I think it's a possibility."

"God," Jody said, sounding devastated by his words. "What can we do?"

"Find out what's going on. What's really going on."

"And how do we do that?"

"Find the babysitter."

"But how?"

"That's the hell of it," David Fairbain said. "I don't have any idea."

4

IN THE WHITE BLAST OF THE CADILLAC'S headlights, Glen Stover hugged his three-year-old daughter Annie, lifting her into his arms.

"It's all right, baby, it's all right," he said, sober now as he stroked her blonde hair. Her pink pajamas were torn and filthy, her backside soaked through with sweat. He could smell and feel the fact that she'd wet herself. Her face was covered with harsh red insect bites.

Marietta ran from the car to where they stood, just on the peak of the small hillock overlooking the large stone manor house below. The house, suspiciously, sat in complete darkness. She threw her arms around her husband and child, collecting them into a tight, protective circle.

"Honey, where's your sister and the babysitter?"

But for the moment all Annie could do was sob so violently that it was terrifying for both her parents to watch.

"Let's get her back to the house," Glen Stover said.

But at that suggestion, Annie began to cry even more furiously.

Frightened now, his mind attacking itself with images of all the fates that could have befallen his oldest daughter, Glen eased Annie's rigid body into Marietta's arms. "I'll go ahead," he said. "See where Hedley is."

Marietta, above Annie's tears, said, "The house is dark. Be careful."

Glen nodded, then started down the narrow dirt path that wound up at the manor home's back door. The night smelled of mint and his own sweat; of impending rain and the Scotch he'd been drinking. The path was pebbled. Twice he nearly fell. He would no longer permit his mind to conjure dire fates for Hedley. He refused to believe that she wasn't inside, and safe.

As he ran, he realized his age and his lack of conditioning. He panted like a dog. He was very thirsty, too.

At the back door, nearly stumbling over a wrapped green snake of garden hose the maintenance man had mistakenly left out today, Glen didn't bother to fumble for his keys. He took off his jacket, wrapped it around his fist, and smashed through a pane of back door glass. He reached in, snapped the deadbolt, and proceeded inside.

Instantly, he knew something was wrong. "Hedley!" he called out. There was no answer. He hadn't really expected one.

As he penetrated deeper into the house, he flipped on lights. The vast house quickly shone with its usual splendor. The three-hundred-year-old Flemish brass chandelier, refitted for electricity, looked almost startling.

He put a hand on the banister, looking at the silken sweep of mahogany that vanished in the shadows of the second floor. A strangeness had settled on the house, one he could not account for, but one that made him feel as if he had mistakenly entered someone else's home.

He called Hedley's name again and went up the stairs, two at a time, panting even more than before.

When he reached the landing, he felt for a light switch on the west wall. From the shadowy glow of a nearby window, he saw his own silhouette—gigantic and menacing—lean in to flip the switch on. Then the shadow was

155

gone and he was looking at rose patterns in the wallpaper surrounding the light switch.

He started his search of all the rooms on the second floor.

In the first three—Annie's, the sewing room, the girls' bathroom—he found nothing untoward. Annie's room was a triumph of disorganization and clutter. Hedley's would be completely different. He allowed himself a momentary smile as he thought of how dissimilar his two girls were.

The library yielded nothing, either. He had begun to wonder frantically if the babysitter might not have been a kidnapper in disguise. He cursed himself for even thinking of having sex with the girl. With Annie in shock and Hedley nowhere to be found, he felt as if his lust had betrayed everything he had ever held dear.

In Hedley's room, he found a mussed bed and a clean, orderly hymn to tidiness. He found no trace of his daughter.

He leaned down to the light blue percale sheet and touched it with his fingers. He felt, or imagined he did, the last fading heat of where Hedley had lain. Terror and rage choked in his throat and his eyes watered over with tears.

When it happened, he was just turning to go back to the hallway and resume his search.

She appeared with no warning whatsoever—no grunt, no quick intake of breath—she simply dove at him and he did not have time to register the sight his eyes tried to deny. He just stood there, unable to move.

Finally, having calmed her some, Marietta sat Annie against the base of an oak tree. She had tried three times to take the girl down the path to the great stone house, but Annie refused.

"It's still in there, Mom," Annie said, her tears giving way now to hiccups and sharp but fewer sobs.

"What's in there, dear?"

"You know."

"No, I don't know."

"It must've been in there all along."

Marietta sighed, kneeling closer to her daughter. "Do you know where Hedley is?"

Annie looked up with large, forlorn eyes and said, "The thing in her room. It got her."

Marietta could not help herself. The way Annie spoke, so deliberately and melodramatically, like a heroine in a bad science fiction movie, Marietta had to smile.

"Now, Annie," she said after thirty seconds.

"Yes."

"I want you to think very hard."

"All right."

"Where did the babysitter go?"

"I don't know, Mom, honest. When I woke up—" The tears were coming back.

Showing an impatience that was not customary, nor very helpful to Annie—an impatience she was immediately ashamed of—she said in the most reasonable manner she could summon, "Annie, I need you to do something for me."

"Do what?"

"I need you to act like a big girl. Do you know how you always say that you wish you were a big girl like Hedley."

"Uh-huh."

"Well, now's your chance to show me."

"What do I have to do?"

"You have to let me stand up, and then you have to stand up, so I can put you in my arms and take you down the path to the house."

"I'm afraid."

"I know you're afraid, Annie. But I won't let anything happen to you. I promise."

"It's still down there."

"Please be a big girl, Annie."

"Can you go down here, and I'll just wait for you and Daddy?"

"I've thought about that, but it's not a good idea to leave you alone."

"Is Daddy in the house?"

"Yes. And he's waiting for us. Look down the hill, Annie. Look at all the lights."

Annie had thus far carefully avoided looking at the manor house. "Are the lights on?"

"Yes, Annie. See for yourself."

"All the lights?"

"Most of the lights, Annie. Most of them. Please take a look."

Slowly, almost ponderously, Annie turned around and stared back down the hill, rubbing a pajama sleeve against her runny nose as she moved. "The lights are on."

"That's what I said, dear. The lights are on."

"And Daddy's in there?"

"Yes, Daddy's in there."

"Do you think it would stay with the lights on?"

Marietta had decided to attribute some of her daughter's words to a nightmare. Something had definitely happened here, but probably not what Annie hinted at. "No, I don't think it would stay with the lights on."

"You promise?"

"Yes, I promise." With that, she leaned in and pressed a clean handkerchief from her purse to the cut on Annie's leg.

"You won't let anything happen?"

"No, dear. I've already explained—" Her patience was being tried again. No matter how much you love a child—

She was just putting on her best patient-mommy face when the screaming started from the stone house down below. She turned around just as Annie had done and stared down at the house.

"See, Mommy," Annie said. "It's still there, just like I told you."

Chapter Six

1

"NOW I WANT YOU TO STAY RIGHT HERE."

"Yes, Mommy."

"No matter what you hear from inside the house, stay right here."

"Yes, Mommy." Pause. "Mommy, I don't want to go in there anyway."

Marietta leaned over and kissed Annie. She sat her daughter in the swing seat of the gazebo, a sentimental touch her husband had added to the grounds the year she turned forty. The gazebo smelled woody from the hard rains of the past few days, and the flowers around it—Russian Sage, Live-Forever Sedums, and Balloon Flowers—joined in lending the night a rich, sweet nostalgia. They should be roasting weiners over a fire instead of—

"Just don't move from here," Marietta said emphatically. There was no other choice but to leave Annie here.

God only knew what Marietta would find inside. There had not been a scream for a minute now.

"Yes, Mommy," Annie said, pulling her injured leg up closer to her and grimacing in the process.

Marietta had already taken off her pumps. It was like her to set them down—even in the midst of all the screaming—carefully by the rock garden so she would remember where to find them. She hated that side of herself.

Pebbles on the path chewed at her feet like tiny fish. A jogger, she easily reached the house and entered it within thirty seconds, calling out her husband's name, hearing only her own echoes in return.

She ran into the living room, bumping against a sharp-edged coffee table, and cursing about it. She almost never cursed. She went through the first floor flipping on lights and moving her eyes around like a security camera, looking for any trace of Glen or Hedley. Aside from a messy sink—a red Jeno's pizza carton resting on the counter—there was no evidence that anybody had been in the house tonight.

Turning her thoughts to upstairs, her fear became almost unbearable. If they were upstairs—and where else could they be?—and hadn't answered any of her calls . . .

Glen kept a pistol somewhere, but right now she wasn't sure where. From a kitchen drawer she took a formidable butcher knife—the same one Glen usually used on Thanksgiving and Christmas—and went back through the house to the staircase.

Swallowing hard, keeping the knife straight out in front of her, she started up the stairs, one careful step after another. She stopped once, thinking she had heard a muffled cry somewhere in the darkness of the second floor. Then she decided it had been the sound of a barn owl, that high peculiar bleating only a barn owl makes, and she went on.

She found him right at the head of the steps.

Not even in the grisliest supermarket tabloids had she ever seen anything like this.

Glen lay sprawled and broken, as if he had been dropped from a great height. His right arm was flung backwards over his left shoulder. His right eye rested like a plump blue bug on the edge of his forehead, the eye slowly sliding off, leaving a trail of slick white pus behind.

The rest of him looked even worse. His heart had been ripped out, leaving a bloody hole, dark and forbidding. His innards had been torn out, too, and now lay in a steaming heap on the floor next to him. They looked as if he had vomited them up.

But always her glance went back, however unwillingly, to the empty socket of his eye. It was so violent a wound, so overwhelming an outrage, that it momentarily killed all fight in her. She couldn't even scream. She leaned back against the wall and began sliding down. She made a small, frail sound, not unlike the one the barn owl had made earlier.

Then she looked up as she heard a noise down the hall. The noise had been the unmistakable one of a human footstep on oaken floor. Since the only light came up from the floor below, she raised her eyes and tried to give shape to somebody moving toward her, coming out of the long dark tunnel of the hallway.

Only gradually did she realize who it was. As the form became familiar, she pushed herself up off her haunches and began sobbing openly, happy that at least her daughter had been spared.

She put her arms out and locked Hedley tight into an embrace. She held her six-year-old daughter as if there were nothing more precious on the earth. And at the moment, nothing was.

"Oh, Hedley," she said, there in the shadowy gloom of the second-floor landing.

She stroked her daughter's hair and held her increasingly tighter, feeling the reassuring softness of Hedley's body pressed against hers. "Oh, Hedley," she said several times, seemingly incapable of saying anything more coherent or meaningful at the moment.

Finally pulling herself together, she said, "We've got to get the police."

She eased herself away from Hedley and took three steps to the light switch on the landing. She turned on the light and then turned back to Hedley.

Her first impression was that Hedley had been torn up as much as her father had been. Her white pajamas were soaked with blood, and you could see purple pieces of ripped flesh clinging to various spots on her body.

It was when she saw Hedley's eyes and fingers that Marietta knew the truth. The word shock occurred to her, but she rejected it at once. While Hedley's blue eyes did seem removed from reality in some way, there was still in her gaze a ferocity, an anger that caused Marietta to step backwards to the wall.

The fingers told the rest of the tale. Blood, flesh, and innards like those on the floor covered and dripped from her hands. Her fingers appeared to have rended open her father's body.

"My God," Marietta said. "Your father—"

In a voice her mother did not recognize, a voice that belonged more properly to a sixty-year-old man, Hedley said, "I don't want to kill you, too, Mother. Let me go. Please."

"Go? But where?" Marietta was in shock, her mind dazed and dull. She looked down at the corpse of her husband—a fly buzzing noisily over the empty eye socket now—and then back at her daughter. As hard as she tried, Marietta could make no sense of this. None.

"Please, Mother," Hedley said again, raising a bloody hand to indicate that she wanted to walk around her mother and down the stairs.

"Hedley, whatever happened—"

Hedley lunged at her then. The look in her eyes was not Hedley's, for Hedley no longer existed. She had become some kind of alien animal, eyes the color of blood, mouth tight and drooling with a dark fluid, hands shaped into stubby claws.

Hedley grabbed her mother's shoulder, ripping away the fabric of the black cocktail dress, the gesture so violent that Marietta was hurled back against the wall in the process.

"Hedley!" she called again, not knowing if she was pleading for mercy or asking her daughter to trust her mother. Probably it was both.

But Hedley had succeeded in doing what she'd wanted. She had maneuvered Marietta away from blocking the stairs. Hedley moved down them confidently, two at a time, down into the light, her auburn hair looking oddly beautiful in the glow from the chandelier.

Marietta struggled to her feet and ran after her. She was afraid that somehow Hedley would find Annie and—

Reaching the front porch, Marietta paused and looked

around. Her eyes had to adjust to the moonlit darkness before they were able to pick out Hedley.

The girl was going in the opposite direction from Annie, into the heavy woods to the east of the house. She certainly seemed to know just where she wanted to go.

Marietta quickly ran back upstairs to her bedroom. Tearing clothes from closet and drawers, she managed to put on a white blouse, jeans, and a pair of Nikes in less than a minute. Then, still buttoning her blouse, she ran down the stairs and back to Annie.

"You're going to have to wait here some more, darling," she said.

"Is Daddy all right?"

She had no choice but to lie. "Yes, he's fine. And so is Hedley. But there's something I have to do, so I have to have your word again that you won't go in the house. All right?" Her words were coming out in convulsive sobs. She was icy with sweat and still vaguely nauseated from what she'd seen on the second-floor landing.

"So do you promise me?"

"I promise, Mommy," Annie said, drawing herself into an even smaller ball on the right side of the big swing chained to the ceiling of the gazebo. Then she said, "My knee still hurts real bad."

"When I get back, Annie, I promise you I'll fix your knee. I promise."

"You going to squirt me with Bactine?"

Marietta leaned forward and kissed her three-year-old on the forehead. She ran back to the house and phoned the police, trying to keep her voice steady. They would, they said, dispatch a car immediately.

Then she took off running, looking desperately for Hedley.

2

AS ANY NUMBER OF HER LOVERS AND BOTH husbands had pointed out, Jody had never been very good at waiting for things. Once when she was a junior in college, she had feared she was pregnant. This was on a gray rainy Easter weekend. Instead of waiting till Monday and the university clinic, Jody took a 1953 Plymouth with two bad tires and only one headlight three hundred miles back home to an intern she'd dated a few times. He gave her good news (not p.g.) and then asked her out for that very same night. In gratitude Jody accepted and they ended up seeing *Hang 'em High,* a Clint Eastwood movie that seemed to stir the intern up quite a lot but that left Jody vaguely depressed. There was just too much violence. She shook hands with the intern after the movie, kissed him once on the cheek, and then climbed into the Plymouth and headed back to the university in time to wear a new pastel blue suit and white pumps dyed to match to Easter Sunday services at First Presbyterian, a rather splendiferous red brick church that had the ability to make Jody feel holy. Then there was the incident of the broken window. Sometime during the malaise of her second marriage, and during the even more difficult malaise of coming to grips with her alcoholism, Jody accidentally smashed the back porch window. She felt so guilty—she'd been drinking and tripped against it and there was just no excuse for her behavior—she walked six miles to a Hardware Hank's and back. Hubby had the only car. Hubby was off somewhere. But damned if she'd give him the satisfaction of seeing what her penchant for liquor had wrought this time.

Now, nine years later, she was waiting for word of her

granddaughter Jenny, and she was no better at all at displaying patience. Not at all.

By this time she had worked out a sort of invisible path that traversed the living room eastward and then back again. Sam was still sleeping, thank God, and David Fairbain was angled boyishly in the recliner next to the end table that held the room's most important object, the telephone.

"You could always sit down," David said.

"Yes, I suppose I could, couldn't I?" She hated herself when she got in these moods.

He said, "Sorry I brought it up." Obviously, she'd hurt his feelings, just exactly what she'd both wanted to do and wanted *not* to do. Things could really get screwed up when you wanted to evoke two opposite responses from one person at the same time. PMS was all she could think of to explain her confusion. Jenny should never have vanished when Jody was about to start her period.

"No, David, I'm the one who's sorry." She paused in her pacing, looking at David across the room. "You're such a help, and I treat you like this."

He grinned. "Jody, you always sort of treated me like that."

"Really?"

"Yes. Really."

"God. Why didn't you slap me or something?"

He sat there, a lot better-looking than he should have been at his age, and said, "I guess I thought I was in love with you, and my folks had always taught me to never slap somebody you really love." He grinned again. "That was a joke."

Her mind still on Jenny, she hadn't gotten it. Now she

offered a weak smile in return and said, "Maybe when this is all over, maybe then I'll laugh."

"We're going to find her, Jody."

"I know you're just saying that. But go right ahead saying it. I mean, it sounds so good."

"It's the truth, Jody."

She was about to start pacing again, but then she said, "Could I ask you to do me a favor?"

"What's that?"

"Come over here and hug me. And I'm not being romantic, David, or coming on to you."

"I understand, Jody. I understand."

So he got up and came over and slid his arms around her waist and took her to him the way a parent takes a sad child, just holding her to his chest, just holding her.

She started crying, crying very softly, there against his chest, and as she did so she thought: this is the only good thing that's happened all day, me being able to cry. Because there were times when she couldn't cry at all. Times a coldness froze her into herself like some prehistoric animal trapped forever in ice, and only tears could melt her prison and free her.

She looked over at the phone and said, "I wish it would ring."

"It'll ring, Jody. It'll ring," David said softly.

"I'm just so scared for her," Jody said. And then the tears really came.

3

ARCHEOLOGISTS CALLED IT AN OSSUARY.
Most folks called it a burial pit.

There was only one way to reach the pit—on foot and
traveling a narrow dirt trail that wound around a clay
mountain and angled down into deep and spiteful undergrowth.

The pit had been discovered by white men in 1903.
Reporters from as far away as Sweden came to examine
its contents. A tall man in a stovepipe hat set his hand-
cranked movie camera to filming the excavation. From
the reservation, James's grandfather had protested what
the white men were doing. As usual with white men, the
words of a red man had no effect.

At the time, it was estimated that the burial pit was
nearly 4,000 years old. Carbon tests fifty years later con-
firmed this judgment. Human bones, animal remains, and
a copper instrument were found in the pit. Even today
there was speculation as to what kind of society these
Indians had lived in. Still, little was known. There remained just the catalog of bones found in the multi-body
grave: skulls, teeth, femurs, a full pelvic girdle, ribs, leg
bones, and the teeth of an animal no one was able to
identify.

On his way down the trail, walking steadily as he did
along the Interstate each day, the Mesquakie Indian saw
a squirrel. He stopped. This would be his offering.

He stood beneath the looming clay mountain, his hunting knife now filling his right hand, crouched so he could
spring at the squirrel that sat in the shadows of a jagged
edge of clay. The brown and white squirrel, standing on

his hind paws, chittered in James's direction, as if warning him away.

James inhaled deeply, smelling the water from the twisting creek a quarter mile away, the dust from the surrounding clay, and the textured aromas of pine, spruce and hardwoods of various kinds. As usual, he permitted himself the fantasy of thinking what this land must have been like before the white men came in their wooden boats from Europe. When ponies without saddles and red men without prison chains roamed these lands and delved into the profound religious truths the lands yielded up only to the red men, the white men being too stupid to look at the truths plainly set out for them . . .

He was quicker than the squirrel. His knife carved a notch in the animal's throat. Blood sprayed over James's face and shirt. Holding the animal in his large hand, he finished the rest of the job, opening up the belly cavity. In the moonlight, the intestines glistened as James made his way down the rest of the trail, a wren in a nearby pine lively suddenly, as if a false dawn had streaked the sky.

In 1929 one of the skulls found in the excavation turned up missing from the state university's archeology department. No less a figure than President Herbert Hoover lent his name to the recovery process. He talked about the "deep historical significance of the burial pit." He talked about growing up in Iowa and watching "the Indians' pride in their past." He talked about a reward that would be jointly paid by the federal and state governments for the safe return of the skull. Shortly thereafter the economy collapsed causing the Great Depression, and Herbert Clark Hoover found himself with far more troublesome problems to handle than the theft of an obscure skull from an obscure burial pit out in the Midwest.

The skull was now back where it belonged, James knew with satisfaction. In the 1950s, his father returned it to its proper place, knowing that the white men had long ago forgotten about it, and knowing that even if they were still searching, they would most likely not look in the excavation sight itself.

James jumped down into the ten-foot-by-ten-foot burial pit, landing hard on his feet. Now the pit was nothing more than hardened clay, an empty bowl in which the occasional bear came to slumber when the red and gold leaves of autumn tore from the trees, and where small animals sometimes ate and peed. No, there was nothing remarkable about the place now at all.

Kneeling, he worked quickly, the damp clay of the floor soaking his trousers. He knew exactly where to begin unpacking the earth. Once, he paused in his work to look up at misty clouds racing past the full moon. He thought of his ancestors thousands of years ago, performing this same ritual.

He thought of his wife's words. That he should never have helped the woman those long years ago.

He thought of their daughter and what had become of her. He shook his head, hating almost everybody he could think of, hating most especially himself.

In all, it took twenty minutes of digging with his fingers, grasping, pulling in the rich red clay. When it was all finished he brought forth the head of a human skeleton, held it up to the moonlight, and appraised it as usual with awe.

Four thousand years ago (so the woman told them) the skull had belonged to a shaman, a magic man, of a tribe that was perhaps the fiercest ever to fight on the great plains in the center of the vast continent. Tokulki his name had been. He taught his fellow tribesmen many truths. He taught that a scalp must be taken, because otherwise your soul can not pass unavenged to heaven. He taught that evil human spirits were often reincarnated into animal spirits. He taught that witches were people inside of whom lizards had taken up living. He taught that the rainbow was nothing more than a gigantic snake which controlled the rain itself.

And he taught about the Spirit-with-the-Head-of-a-Grasshopper, the Indian woman who did not know consciously that she was the darkest of Indian goddesses, her fate on earth always the same, to bear children of her own kind who would be taken from her and ultimately killed. The Indian woman's name was Witsah and given her desire for revenge, she was one of the most terrifying of spirits Tokulki knew.

Time had worn a large hole in the head of the skeleton. It was here that James dumped the innards of the squirrel, still hot and juicy-looking.

As always, James had dragged down a flat piece of stone he kept hidden under the undergrowth on the lip of the pit. The altar was the resting place for the head of Kujani, the interlocutor between Witsah and all the dark powers of the known universe.

Less than two minutes after James had poured the sacrifice into the skull, Kujani, the interlocutor, began screaming.

There was no accounting for the sound and it always horrified James, despite his deep reverence for the ways of the red man. He fell back against the clay wall, slamming his hands over his ears, waiting for the screaming to stop.

In the gloom, James could see the blood beginning to

pour from the holes in the skelton's face, from the eyes, from the nose, from the mouth. The blood was thick and smelled ironlike. It came in an unceasing torrent, spreading out over the clay earth, soon reaching James. The screaming sounded like that of a small animal in the final moments of painful death (James had seen a wild dog die this way and had never forgotten it). The screaming continued.

From his pocket, and moving fast now, James took a small plastic bottle, the kind pharmacists use. He knelt next to the makeshift stone altar and set the clear plastic bottle before the skull, so that some of the blood flowing from it would fill the bottle.

The screaming stopped abruptly. It usually did.

Then James was left with only the soft wind and the smell of clay and mint leaves and the sound of rabbits and possums in the tangled undergrowth.

Picking up the bottle and capping it, he bent over and began the process of reburying the skull.

Kujani must have been satisfied, otherwise he would not have yielded up the blood.

It took ten minutes to repack the skull inside the clay.

Then, with the blood safely in the vial, James returned to the cabin to complete his part of the bargain he had made long ago with the Indian woman he now knew to be Witsah, the spirit-with-the-head-of-a-grasshopper.

4

"THERE MAY BE SOME NEWS ABOUT YOUR granddaughter. At this point we can't be sure, but I need to check what she was wearing again."

Jody gave the officer on the phone a description of the clothes Jenny was wearing.

The officer said, "It could be her then. The caller wasn't sure about the apparel, but it does sound quite a bit like your granddaughter."

"Where was she seen?"

"Up near High Rock. You know where that is?"

"Sure. Up in the clay hills."

"Umm-hmm. A little west of there, actually."

"You've sent cars already?"

"Yes, ma'am."

"Is there anything I can do?"

"I know it's tempting, ma'am, but the best thing you can do is sit tight."

Ordinarily, being called ma'am would have bothered Jody. But not now. Not tonight.

David stood next to her, tense as she was, holding one of her hands as she spoke.

"Are you going to check in pretty often?"

"As often as we can, ma'am. I can't say when the first report will be. We've got several men up near the hills now."

"Is there anything else around there these days?"

"Ma'am?"

"Anything that might attract a young girl. An amusement park, perhaps, something like that."

"Not that I know of, ma'am."

"Then why would she go off walking up there?"

174

"I'm afraid I can't answer that, ma'am."

She knew she was getting hysterical. There were tears in her voice. She didn't give a damn. "Is there any average on youngsters who return?"

"Ma'am?"

"Do one out of two come back again safely?"

"Oh. I see. I'm not sure."

"I thought I'd ask."

"Is someone there with you, ma'am?"

"Yes. My daughter and my friend."

"If you don't mind my saying so, ma'am, why don't you sit down and ask one of them to make you some tea or something."

"I see."

"Ma'am?"

"I meant I see what you're saying. I'm sorry, officer, but this is difficult for me."

"I understand, ma'am."

"I appreciate your concern."

"Quite all right."

"You'll call then?"

"The minute we get anything new."

"Thanks, officer. Thanks very much."

"You just sit down and let your daughter and your friend help you through this. All right?"

"Yes."

Jody hung up, slipping her hand out of David's, going over to the fabric-bare couch and sitting in the far corner all by herself. She began sobbing without any warning at all. David came over and was about to sit down with her but she waved him away. He went over by the television and stood watching her. She continued to cry like this for five minutes. David stared down at the TV screen occasionally, watching the images change from sitcom stars to local news anchors.

She got up as abruptly as she'd sat down. She said not a word to him. She went into the kitchen and flipped the overhead light inside of which were encased perhaps two million dead mosquitos and moths. She took the Have A Good Day pad that had been magnetically affixed to the freezer part of the refrigerator and wrote a note to Sam.

She tore the note from the pad with a real ferocity. She handed it over her shoulder where she knew David to be. "Would you read that for me and tell me if it's clear?"

"Sure."

He read it and handed it back. "As a bell," he said. "But I'm not sure it's the right thing."

"I didn't ask you to go along."

"No, but I'm going anyway."

She turned around and drew him near enough to hug. She did not want to start crying again. Not now. "Good," she said. "I don't know what I'd have done if you hadn't offered."

A minute later they were in his car and headed for the section of the city called High Rock.

5

ONCE SHE HAD NOT BEEN FAT. ONCE HER hair had not been gray. Once men looked at her with lust rather than loathing. In those days, five decades ago, her name had not been the ludicrous Helen but instead Hanging Flower. Her mother, the first woman to ever assume a full position on the tribal council, and a woman who had not let her gender keep her back, had posited the fantasy that Hanging Flower was a direct descendent of another Hanging Flower, a true Apache princess discovered by a *New York Times* reporter in 1886. Those on the tribal council had agreed to this fantasy without question, as did most others on the reservation. Hanging Flower and her mother had, after all, come from somewhere vague in the Southwest. These were Plains Indians starved for any kind of romance amidst the tin buildings and poverty of the reservation. Even if Hanging Flower was a make-believe princess, she was better than nothing.

The name Helen came when she was twenty years old, from a white man who felt her Indian name was embarrassing. You could not blame Hanging Flower for her self-delusion. Her mother had cultivated the princess myth so carefully and so well that of course Hanging Flower herself believed it. For one thing, she *looked* like a princess: dark eyes, a beautifully shaped nose, a small but inviting mouth, and the high cheekbones the white women in the nearby town envied so much (she knew this because white women would often stop Hanging Flower on the street and then talk about her as if she wasn't there, as if they were assessing a doll rather than a human being). Too, there was her body, a graceful and supple body, high small breasts and very long legs. Since the myth and her looks had intrigued the reservation for all the years of her girlhood, Hanging Flower assumed that she would ultimately do well among the white people. The day of her twentieth birthday, she bade both her mother and the reservation good-bye. With the blessings of the white man who oversaw the reservation, she moved to Winthrop, took a three dollar a week sleeping room, and got a job in the basement of the Woolworth's store as a clerk. She was an instant success, and in the ways that mattered, too. Daily, especially during the hot summer months, white boys from good families came to the Woolworth's basement to flirt with her in ways sometimes crude, but more often subtle and nervous. She might have been a frail fawn they'd discovered at roadside. Not that there weren't complaints from older white customers who could see what was going on. They felt this was scandalous. Then she met the Hughes kid, as he was invariably called, during her second summer in the midst of the whites, and the first summer she felt bold enough to be on the arm of a white boy. The Hughes kid (whose age was twenty-two and whose real name was Robert) was the son of the local newspaper editor, a man held by all to be far more liberal than the people his paper served. His liberalism died apparently when he saw his son with Hanging Flower. He became adamant about breaking up the couple. Their biggest problem was that they were genuinely in love. But he broke them up anyway. It was then—as she looked back at it now—that she began her drinking. It was not so obvious at first. What *was* obvious, however, was that her taste in men degenerated. She began hanging out with the type of white men you met in white bars. They were not gentle and respectful and quietly curious as the Hughes boy had been. Instead they were often rude and hostile and demanding. But they had money and they wanted her and that came to be all that mattered. As long as there was alcohol, as long as there was noise.

She met her husband outside of such a place. A white man had slapped her. The Indian man, apparently walking by in the shadows, saw this and came over and jerked her from the grasp of the white man. She had been very drunk and sobbing (she knew by this time that alcohol would be her curse). He carried her back to his cabin where for three days he forced simple but good food down her (she came to share his taste for squirrel meat, especially the meat from the breast) and told her of the evils of the white man and the white man's liquor. She never fell in love with him—he was homely, he was strange, he was impossible to understand—but she never left him either (except for adulterous forays which were at least as difficult for her as they were for him). She stayed at the cabin and fixed up some curtains and went into town and got a hooked rug and some pine boards for shelving and began to make them a home. For the first time since leaving the reservation, she felt protected. She married him on a hard November day when the overcast sky had the same effect on her mood as her period did. But she married him and lived with him and felt for at least a year that she had disposed of her alcohol problem. Then one day she stopped, on her long walk back from shopping, in a bar. She did it on impulse, not certain what she would do inside. She quickly learned what she would do inside. She would do what she had always done inside. She would drink and find herself drawn to the meanest white man in the place. That night her husband found her around midnight. With abiding sadness, he brought her home. The white man had given her a black eye. On her breasts (they had gone out into his car) you could see his teeth marks.

It was shortly after this that she learned of what lay in the basement. One night as she tried to sleep she heard wailing noises. At first she assumed the sounds belonged to an injured animal outside. But then she realized that they came from the basement and they were not those of an animal, not exactly anyway. Around midnight, she saw silhouetted in the doorway a young Winthrop girl. She wondered what a young white girl, maybe ten years of age, would be doing out here at midnight. She soon learned. Her husband guided the girl in and then silently guided her down the trapdoor leading to the basement level that Hanging Flower had never seen. Soon, the cries of the little girl intermingled with the wailing sound of what lay below. Hanging Flower, unable to stand it any longer, rushed to the trapdoor, wanting to rescue the girl. "No," her husband had said. "She would just kill us." "Who would kill us?" Hanging Flower had asked. And so her husband told her about the creature in the basement. Hanging Flower realized, in listening to him, how singular his hatred of white people was. He had only agreed to help the woman because she would prey on innocent young girls. White girls. In the ensuing days, Hanging Flower thought of going into Winthrop and talking to the police. In fact, she twice set off on foot to do just that. But finally she gave up trying, because her husband was her only friend. She was grateful to him even if she found him increasingly repulsive and unknowable. She went back to drinking and he did not stop her. Indeed, he seemed to encourage her. It was a way to keep her weak. It let him have the ultimate power over her, and it allowed her the proper distraction from the creature in the basement.

All these long years later, she sat now on the porch of the cabin and watched for him. Downstairs, the wailing sound as well as the cries of the little girl had ceased and Hanging Flower knew that the creature had claimed another victim. She wondered if there had been more than five victims over the years. She wondered why she had started helping him, as she had tonight, escorting the girls into the basement, letting the creature—

But now Hanging Flower had begun to think of all the ways that white people had spurned her over the years. Now helping her husband did not seem so bad.

Swigging from the Jim Beam, she kept her shining brown eyes alert as the young girl walked up to the cabin.

"Evening, honey," Hanging Flower said.

The girl was probably about seven, Hanging Flower decided. Her white pajamas were soaked with sweat and blood, stained with green from where she'd apparently fallen.

The girl's eyes were dull and you could tell by the way she cocked her head, as if listening to distant music, that she was hearing the buzzing sound the creature in the basement always filled their ears with.

"What's your name, honey?"

At first, the girl looked at her uncomprehendingly. Licking dry lips, the girl finally said, "Hedley."

Hanging Flower snorted. "Hedley? That's a funny name." But Hanging Flower knew it was also another kind of name—the kind of name that belonged to a *rich* young white girl. Hanging Flower's eyes narrowed. "You know why you came here, honey?"

Hedley nodded. She seemed to be on the verge of tears.

"The thing is, don't give her any trouble. You understand?"

Again Hedley nodded.

"You give her any trouble, she'll give you trouble. You know what I'm talking about?"

For only the second time, the frail young girl spoke. "I'm afraid."

"They all are, honey," Hanging Flower laughed, starting to resent this rich young white girl all over again. The Jim Beam had just kicked in on a much higher level. "Now, I'm going to take you inside and you'll go downstairs. All right?"

"All right."

"And you ain't going to give me no problems?"

Hedley shook her straight auburn hair. You could see where dirt had smudged her forehead. She reminded Hanging Flower of a sentimental painting of a waif.

Hanging Flower held out her bottle. "You want some? Maybe it'll help."

Hedley stared at the bottle. "No thank you."

Hanging Flower laughed again. "Guess you are a little young." She stood up and said, "Come on."

Hanging Flower had turned around and started to open the door. She sensed that the girl had not moved. When Hanging Flower turned around again, she discovered that she was right.

Hanging Flower had to fight what she felt just then. Hedley looked so lost and vulnerable, that not even her hatred of whites could keep Hanging Flower from feeling sorry for her. She momentarily considered the idea of letting Hedley go, but then she thought of the one time she'd considered such a course—how she'd awakened later in the night to find that the thing in the basement had come upstairs to pay her a visit. Hanging Flower had never seen the creature before. She would never forget the threat the creature had telepathically put into her head—*You are to help me or I will make you like them.* By "them," the creature obviously meant the young girls.

Leaning against the door, wiping spilled whiskey from her hand on to her red peasant skirt, Hanging Flower said, "I'd help you if I could, honey, but I can't. Now you get up here, all right?"

Still Hedley didn't move.

"Honey, we got to go. We got to move it."

Already the wailing had begun in the basement. The creature knew Hedley was out here. The creature was ready. Hungry now.

"Now, come on."

When Hedley still did not move, Hanging Flower shoved the uncapped pint in the elastic band of her skirt and proceeded down the steps, where she took Hedley crossly by a thin shoulder and pushed her toward the porch. "You're gonna make this hard for yourself, honey. It's just what I told you that you don't want to do."

She gave Hedley another shove. Hedley tripped, sprawling over the porch.

"Damn," Hanging Flower said. "I didn't want that to happen. I really didn't."

She went up to Hedley, helped the girl to her feet. She tried not to notice the girl's silent tears or the fear in her eyes. Much as she tried, she couldn't hate this little girl.

Hanging Flower sighed and put out her hand. "Sometimes this helps. Sometimes I hold their hands till they disappear down the ladder. All right?"

Hedley nodded.

Hanging Flower led her gently inside, past the smells of fried potatos and the two sour cots on which man and wife had long slept separately and the tiny eleven-inch Sears color TV set.

Hanging Flower always got winded whenever she had to bend over and pull up the trapdoor. When you weighed what she did, any kind of exaggerated movement was difficult.

But she got the door open fine, standing back quickly as always because of the cold and the smell of decay that had been flash frozen in the chill. Even the air from the basement seemed blacker than normal night air.

When Hedley went through, one of her pajama sleeves got caught on the door catch and tore.

Hanging Flower felt sorry for her. She put out her hand again and said, "I'm afraid it's time, honey. I'm afraid it's time."

6

FORTY-FIVE MINUTES EARLIER, MARIETTA Stover had struck her head against a low-hanging tree branch, raising a painful knob on her forehead. The blow was enough to make her lose sight of her daughter, whom she'd glimpsed in the moonlight, cresting a hill, perhaps a quarter mile away.

After being briefly disoriented, Marietta resumed her search, cutting through timberland alive with animal life she couldn't see. Mud from the recent rain smelled acrid in her nostrils and stuck like flypaper on the soles of her shoes. She suffered every kind of bite imaginable, from mosquitos to chiggers, but she scarcely noticed them. All she could recall were the twin images now stamped forever in her memory—that of her husband lying on the landing disemboweled and that of her daughter Hedley with a hand covered in her own father's blood and entrails.

She pushed on. There was nothing else to do. The mud grew deeper, the bites more nasty, the night darker and darker as she penetrated the clay hills and the deep forest surrounding them. Somewhere ahead was Hedley. Somewhere.

By the time she reached the hill that overlooked a steep clay incline, she was almost nauseated from her headache. She did not see the cabin at first. It blended too well with the shadows to be seen easily. But as she stood there, her eyes trying to adjust to the sweep below, she began to recognize the shape of a ragged cabin made of leftover lumber and tin scraps.

Perhaps someone in the cabin had seen Hedley pass by . . .

The incline was even steeper than she'd thought at first and cost her several more bumps and bruises from the hard rutted clay. In all, it took over ten minutes and her headache was now virtually blinding.

She could smell the cabin long before she drew abreast of it. The odors were sickening—rotting food, a chemical toilet, a pile of indeterminate junk to the west of the slanting structure. And something else, too—something almost exotic in its putrescence. To approach the cabin further, she had to cover her mouth and nose with her hand.

When she walked up on the porch, the whole cabin pitched leftward. She had the momentary impression that it would quickly capsize, like a fragile boat in rough waters. She had raised her hand to knock when the Indian woman appeared.

Marietta could never recall being physically afraid of a woman before. Men, yes, but no woman had ever seemed especially threatening to her. But this one was different. Her ragged clothes, the odors that accompanied her, the pint bottle she took from the band of her peasant skirt, the wild gray hair that stuck out from her head like electrified dreadlocks—she was absolutely terrifying.

"What the hell do you want?" the Indian woman demanded.

"I'm looking for my daughter," Marietta said.

"What the hell would your daughter be doing here?"

"I don't mean she came here. I thought you might have seen her pass by. She's very pretty and little. She's six years old." Marietta's voice rose near the end of this. You could hear hysteria building inside her.

"I didn't see her."

"Could anybody else in the house have seen her?"

"House?" the Indian woman sneered. "You think this is a house? Why don't you try shanty. That's the word you want. House." This time when she pronounced the word, she spat off the side of the porch.

Watching the woman spit, Marietta drew within herself. Everything was out of skew. Nothing tonight made sense. *Her husband lying sprawled on the floor. Her daughter standing in front of her with bloody, talonlike hands.* But it was obvious this bitter, drunken Indian woman was going to be no help to her.

Marietta grimaced, sighed, and turned to go, when she saw something lying on the floor that seemed out of place. A piece of white material.

Before the Indian woman knew what Marietta was doing, or could stop her, Marietta took four long strides on the porch and jerked the material free of the latch. Horrible recognition filled her—panic set her heart to a painful pounding. She saw the piece of material torn from Hedley's pajama cuff. There was no doubt it was Hedley's. Her white pajamas were monogrammed on chest and sleeve cuffs: HS.

Almost in shock, Marietta said, "She's here, isn't she?"

"I don't know what the hell you're talkin' about."

"She's here. My daughter's here."

"You get the hell off my property."

Marietta, knowing she would have to get inside the cabin to learn the real truth, snapped back the door and took one step across the threshold. The odors of the place overwhelmed her. Nausea made her wobbly.

She saw a shack of two cots, a kerosene stove, a jumble of chairs, and boxes of canned food goods. But no sign of her daughter.

She turned back to the Indian woman whom she could feel right behind her. "Where is she! Where is my daughter!" By now, Marietta was shrieking. She did not care.

Then she heard the noise. A wailing sound, it came from below. When Marietta looked at the Indian woman again, she saw that for the first time the woman seemed anxious. Apparently the wailing sound was significant.

"Where's the basement door?" Marietta demanded. When, after ten seconds, the Indian woman had not spoken, Marietta shouted, "Where's the basement door?"

She fell to her hands and knees there in the smelly gloom of the tiny cabin. Obviously she was searching for some kind of trapdoor. Within half a minute, she found the outlines of such a door hidden beneath a hooked rug.

She had just put her hand inside the ring that would pick the door up when the Indian woman grabbed her with the force of a wrestling bear. The Indian woman got Marietta in a choke hold and jerked her to her feet. She hurled Marietta across the floor into a cot. The Indian woman rushed over and hit Marietta on the face. Her punch had the strength of a man's.

The Indian woman leaned in and began choking Marietta there on the cot. Her hands were huge and powerful. Marietta had no idea what to do. She took the heel of her hand and placed it against the jut of the Indian woman's jaw and pushed. Then she took her foot and placed it against the Indian woman's abdomen and kicked. While both these moves had some effect on the Indian woman, neither was strong enough to unlock the Indian woman's hands.

Marietta began to understand through her heaving breath and spinning vision that she would soon be unconscious, and soon after that dead.

Letting her body begin to slide off the cot, Marietta got in position to do more damage with her feet. She knew she would have no more than one chance, so she had to make it good. When she had slid halfway to the floor, she brought her right foot up high and hard, catching the Indian woman squarely on the jaw. The choke hold opened. Marietta quickly jumped to her feet.

A few minutes earlier, she had noticed a butcher knife over by a tin bucket used as a sink. She went for it now, keeping her back to it so the Indian woman, who was cursing drunkenly and trying to reorient herself, would not know what Marietta was doing.

As the Indian woman lunged at her again, Marietta's fingers found the knife and quickly brought it around in front of her, just in time to impale the other woman deeply on the upraised knife.

The Indian woman screamed, blood blooming in an already widening pool on the chest of her gray peasant blouse. She tottered in front of Marietta for a moment, as if she could not yet believe what Marietta had done to her, at once accusing, and at the same time pitiful at the end of her life. Then she fell over backwards, blood beginning to bubble from her mouth. Marietta had no doubt she was dead. The butcher knife still rode her heart.

Marietta scrambled for the trapdoor. Somewhere down there was Hedley. She knew it.

On her hands and knees, her hand once again in the door ring, she had just started to pull the trapdoor up when, behind her, she heard the screen door open.

There, silhouetted, stood a tall Indian man. He glanced quickly around the room and saw what had happened. As he stood there, he began to twitch.

Finally, as if breaking through his initial nightmare reaction, he went to the Indian woman on the floor and took her in his arms, embracing her as if she were the most precious infant on the earth.

All Marietta could do was watch. She knew better than to make a move.

The Indian began sobbing once he realized that there was no life in the body he held. He raised his eyes to Marietta. His gaze was more frightening than any weapon she had ever seen.

"So you want to know what's in the basement," he said. He spoke slowly, carefully, as if uncertain of his English. Gently, he laid the dead woman back on the floor. Carefully, he rose to his feet. Easily, he took from his right trouser pocket what appeared to be a small brown medicine bottle. "Now you'll see, white woman. Now you'll see what's in the basement."

He moved with quick grace over to Marietta and kicked her hard on the side of the head, slamming her skull back against a two-by-four used on the wall behind.

The man knelt down, grabbed her wrist, and yanked her to his side. He opened the trapdoor. Unimaginably cold black air came up from the basement. The odors were nearly intolerable.

"Hedley!" she cried. "Hedley!"

"You want to see your daughter?" the Indian said. "The way I just saw my wife?"

Enraged with his own words, he dragged Marietta over to the opening and pushed her down. She clung to the opening with her fingers. He stomped on her hand with his boot heel. He didn't use the steps with her. He simply dropped her.

When the force of her falling body met the resistance of an earthen floor packed hard, Marietta screamed . . .

Then she saw the door being closed and heard a padlock clicking into place.

She was in the darkness now, completely.

Knowing she needed to sit up, she got on her hands and knees, and tried to find out the source of the eerie green glow.

Apparently, it came from beyond a wide bend shaped from the clay of the basement. The place reminded her of a cave. She crawled on her hands and knees around this bend and stopped.

"My God," she said aloud in the sudden silence of the basement.

In the center of the green glow was the upright body of a woman dressed in the Indian buckskins of long ago. But instead of a woman's head, an enormous grasshopper's projected from the creature's shoulders. A young girl Marietta did not recognize held the creature's right hand. Holding on to the left outstretched hand was Hedley. It was easy enough to see the process here. A red bloodlike fluid was flowing from the creature into the veins of the young girls on either side of her. You could see the veins in their wrists swell with the feeding. Neither the creature nor the girls seemed to be conscious. The feeding had put them in some kind of reverie.

"You made a mistake coming here."

When Marietta whirled to confront the speaker, she knew in that instant that the voice belonged to somebody familiar.

Nikki, tonight's babysitter, stood there in front of her, hands on hips.

"What did you do to my husband and my daughter?"

Nikki smiled. "Why don't you ask me what your husband almost did to me."

"Who is that woman?" Marietta said. "And what's she doing—"

For the first time, Nikki showed anger, even contempt. "That woman is my mother. And she is doing to your daughter, and the daughter of others, what the authorities did to my mother and me long ago." She went on, talking quickly for the next two minutes, about what had been going on in Winthrop these past decades.

Marietta listened, numb.

Nikki dropped her head suddenly and reached up over her spine and down the nape of her neck. It took only a few moments. The beautiful young face she had once possessed was torn away now to reveal the same shape as the one perched on her mother's shoulders.

Nikki started moving toward Marietta. Moving very quickly.

Marietta began to edge backward. All she could think of was Hedley's lifeless face as she was connected in some fashion to the ancient creature. The fluid pumping into her veins . . .

Nikki jumped at her just then, sending Marietta tumbling onto the hard earth beneath her, wedged tightly between the wall and a jutting boulder.

In the green glow, Marietta could see a strawlike tube emerging from Nikki's mouth.

Marietta, having no doubt what the tube would be used for, screamed . . .

Chapter Seven

1

THEY HAD BEEN WALKING FOR AN HOUR now, around the periphery of the deep timber that encircled the chain of red clay hills that the locals called mountains. Because a good share of the timberland had been reclaimed by the state two decades earlier, there were dozens of mercury vapor lights to guide their way. Jody had gotten hoarse early on, calling Jenny's name into the night as if she were firing up flares.

Nothing.

Slick with sweat, out of breath from climbing up the 45-degree hills, they moved over now to the part of the forest that ran parallel with the Huntington River. Cars roared by on the throughway, teenagers tossing out beer cans and curses, children with gigantic Dairy Queen cones that threatened to topple under their own weight, elderly couples locked tight within the air-conditioned confines of their carefully kept retirement cars.

It would be so nice to be a child sometimes, Jody thought. Or even an elderly person with a good life behind you, and something like contentment in your heart.

"You okay?" David asked.

She laughed softly, wiping sweat from her forehead. "You read me like radar, as an old boyfriend of mine used to say."

David shrugged. "I grew up in a household where people didn't communicate verbally very well. I learned to read faces."

"That probably comes in handy."

He smiled. "Sometimes I don't like what I see."

Jody was about to say something, but she stopped when they reached the crest of a hill and saw at its bottom a Quick Trip store. "Maybe we should stop and get a Coke or something."

"You're not going to hear me argue about that."

They went down, another carload of teenagers and ugly horn sounds accompanying them. The closer they drew, the more the store reminded her of an optical illusion. There was nothing but timberland and a few scattered park benches out here. The store, almost lurid white and red in the gloom, looked faintly satanic, a lure devised to trap people like Jody and David Fairbain.

"This will give me a chance to call Sam, too," Jody said.

"You think she'll be awake?"

"She's taken these pills before. They usually knock her out for about three or four hours. Then she wakes up."

"Aren't there stronger pills?"

"Unfortunately, she's built up a tolerance to every kind

of sleeping pill there is. If they give her stronger dosages, she may become a pill junkie."

"The poor kid."

Jody's jaw tightened, all her parental guilt flooding back. *If only I'd been a better mother—*

There were a few teenagers playing Donkey Kong, an old man in fuchsia Bermuda shorts, a Chicago Cubs T-shirt, and flapping rubber sandals going for milk from the steamed-over glass milk case, and a coughing man at the counter buying a carton of Camel filters.

After the coughing man left, David went up to the counter and began asking the clerk questions.

Jody went over to the phone, deposited thirty-five cents and called Sam.

Sam answered on the first ring. "Yes?" she said almost breathlessly.

"It's me, honey."

"Did you find her?" Sam's voice was a perfect fusion of dread and hope.

"Not yet, honey. But we're going to. I promise." Pause. "I was just checking to see if the police called."

"No. Not yet."

"How are you doing?"

"I just woke up about fifteen minutes ago."

"Why not lie on the couch and try to get some more sleep? That way you can be next to the phone."

"I'll try . . ."

"I'm sorry, honey."

"I know."

"But we *are* going to find her."

Sam sighed. "Where are you?"

Jody explained. While she talked, she angled her head to see what David Fairbain was doing.

The chubby clerk in the zip-up Quick Trip jacket was just now handing him a piece of paper. The clerk then carefully told David about something and David just as carefully wrote it down. Given the long strokes, more like drawing than writing, Jody suspected David was drawing a map.

"When are you coming back?" Sam asked.

"Are you afraid to be alone?"

"I just don't want you to wear yourself out, Mother. You're not as—"

Jody laughed gently. "Don't start that old lady routine with me again, all right?"

"I just meant—"

"I know, honey. But I'll be fine."

"It's so hot. Heat can wear you down."

"I'll be fine."

After she hung up, she went over to the counter where David waved the white piece of paper at her. She followed him out the front door where they stood in a noisy buzz of mosquitos and moths hurling themselves at the large red and white neon squares, and where the sharp odor of gas was almost intoxicating on such a hot night.

"The clerk in there is a backpacker," David explained, showing her the map. "He knows this forest and these hills very well. He showed me a shortcut that will take us all the way to the hills."

"I'd just like to get going."

He slid his arm around her shoulder and kissed her on the forehead. "We're going, we're going," he said.

Fifteen minutes later they found themselves on a narrow path so filled with low-hanging tree branches and chest-high undergrowth that Jody had the sense that they were lost already.

The other problem with the path was that it curved every fifty feet or so. You couldn't get a look at what was ahead. There was always another sharp turn. This and the deep shadows of the forest enhanced Jody's sense of claustrophobia. But whenever she felt a slight flutter of panic in her chest, she thought of Jenny. The image of Jenny kept her going.

At one point they reached a wide creek, silver in the moonlight shattered by the boughs of scrub pine. Rusty cans jutted up from the shallow water. A plump frog noted their passage by croaking three times in his best bass.

The clay hills rose before them, just beyond a windbreak of more scrub pine. Given their height and slender peaks, the hills really did look like mountains.

"You want to rest a little while?"

"I'd rather just keep on going."

"Fine. But those hills are going to be difficult."

"I'll make it."

"I didn't mean to offend you, Jody."

"You didn't. I'm getting a small headache and that always makes me crabby. No big deal."

They continued onward.

The hills were even more difficult to climb than David had predicted. Rains had left the clay surface muddy and difficult to dig into. Jody slipped backwards twice, covering herself in mud as she did so. The second time, fearing she was going to tumble all the way down into the shallow ravine below, she screamed.

2

MARIETTA TOUCHED A WARM, SLOWLY SEEP-
ing wound near her temple. The sensation—blood has a
texture—made her weak momentarily. But she knew
where she was—the basement—and what she must do
. . . Escape.

Pushing herself to her feet, she saw Nikki suddenly
appear and lunge toward her with a sharp-edged spade.

Marietta scarcely had time to move out of the way as
the spade came clanging down, her own shadow huge in
the green glow on the wall behind her.

The second time she sprang at Marietta, the older
woman was ready, kicking a foot out at the precise instant Nikki bent for better leverage with the shovel.

Nikki, tripping, went sprawling, the spade clanging
away and resting against a chunk of rock.

Marietta dove for the spade, gripping it so tight its
wooden handle chewed into her soft palms.

Nikki was getting to her feet, her grotesque head bob-
bing on her frail shoulders.

Marietta used the spade like a spear, driving it deep
into Nikki's chest.

Nikki, making a noise that was both pathetic and dis-
gusting, fell backwards against the wall.

Marietta jerked the spade from the girl's chest, from
the bloody hole in her chest, only to drive it in deeper a
second time.

Nikki, flailing, collapsed.

Pulling the spade from Nikki's chest once again, Marietta twisted around completely and took four steps to the
creature that held Hedley captive through the tubelike
apparatus.

Bringing the spade down with all her fury, Marietta tried to sever the connection between girl and creature. Generous puking splashes of green fluid ran down the creature and flooded the floor.

That was when Nikki came up from the floor, startling Marietta.

Marietta screamed just before she once more plunged the spade into Nikki's chest, this time killing her . . .

When he heard the scream, he was still upstairs.

He was about to take the brown plastic medicine bottle into the basement. The wailing was starting again. It was time. He knew how she got.

But somehow he could not move.

He sat at the small, wobbly table staring down at the sprawled and broken form of his wife. The knife was still in her.

At the scream, he looked up. The sound was reasonably close.

People. Coming here.

He looked back at his wife. She had died Helen, no longer Hanging Flower. She died with the white man's liquor in her belly and the white man's powder sachet on her fleshy cheeks.

Without realizing it, he began to cry, abrupt sobs that threatened to choke him. He made a huge fist of his right hand and brought it down on the table, splitting the wood viciously.

Slowly, he pushed himself to his feet, the sobs still in his throat, and went to the screen door.

The scream in the hills had echoed for two minutes now, trapped in the tree branches and foliage and clay hills. He wondered who had screamed and why.

As he stood there, he realized that he did not have to wonder why any longer.

Two people, a man and a woman, appeared on the muddy slope of a small clay hill less than a quarter mile away. They were white people of course. Both of them pointed at his cabin and began talking.

He knew he did not have much time.

In his pocket, the blood he had taken from the animal at the burial site seemed almost searingly warm. Ready.

He went quickly to the trapdoor, unlocked the padlock, flung the door open, and started down the stairs.

He had gone seven steps down when he heard the panting sounds. He glanced over his shoulder quickly. In the green glow from the woman on the wall, he saw the girl.

She lay, arms flung wide, on the earthen floor. A pointed shovel had been jammed into her chest, just as a knife had been jammed into Hanging Flower's chest.

Marietta tore the shovel from Nikki's chest and swung it at his back, catching him sharply on the spine.

He jumped down, narrowly avoiding a lethal swing aimed at his head. The shovel made a metallic jarring sound as it banged against the metal ladder.

Facing the white woman now, he pulled from inside his belt a Bowie knife he spent at least an hour a day sharpening. "You bitch," he said.

He got the knife in his hand, balanced it for throwing, and prepared himself for the pleasure he would take from watching and hearing the knife tear into her white breast.

"You bitch," he said again.

She at least had the intelligence to look scared, to understand that her shovel was no match for his Bowie knife.

3

"I DIDN'T KNOW ANYTHING ABOUT THIS place," David said at the same time that James moved toward Marietta, as they moved through sun-baked buffalo grass toward the cabin. The moon was full and silver. "The first I'd ever heard of it was when the clerk back there mentioned it."

"I remember it," Jody said, "from when we used to play up here. There's a really nasty Indian who lives there with his wife. When my cousin Allan was seven, the Indian man grabbed him for trespassing and nearly choked him to death. He's not very fond of white people. He probably won't be willing to help us at all."

"I'm sure that once we explain—"

"Anybody who would choke a seven-year-old isn't real likely to worry about lending a helping hand."

"Maybe he's mellowed some." He smiled at her. "You have."

It was then they heard the sound. Jody's arms were chilled with gooseflesh immediately. Her stomach knotted. "My God," she said. "What was that?"

"It almost sounds like an animal caught in a trap."

"Where did it come from?"

"I'm not sure," David said. "But I've got an idea."

He pointed straight ahead to the cabin.

4

HE HAD NEVER ENJOYED THIS PART OF THE task. There was a puckered, leathery slit, like the mouth of a very old person, on the side of the creature's grass-hopper-shaped head. It was here that the sacrificial blood he had taken from the squirrel tonight had to be poured. He had never gotten used to the spongy quality of the creature's flesh, nor the acrid odor of its body.

"What is that, anyway?" asked the white woman. He'd tied her to a support post.

He turned and looked at her. "You would not under-stand, you bitch."

"Please, I just want to know what's going on." She could not take her eyes from her daughter, whose veins were still being filled with fluid from the Indian woman's.

So he told her.

He still remembered the night, fifty-some years ago, of the transformation.

She had asked of him three things: first, he was to get men from the reservation to dig out a basement from the clay earth beneath the cabin; then he was to help her secure the proper sacrifice (the first of which was the embryo of a human baby; he had killed a three-month pregnant check-out girl he saw every day at Dutch's Foodorama); and last, he was to kidnap her seventeen-year-old daughter back from the orphanage. He had done all these things and she had surprised him, shocked him really, by becoming the creature she was now, a creature bent on bringing harm to the young girls of Winthrop in repayment for what the town had done to her and her daughter. She did not kill the girls—that would have been merciful—but she put them into a state of anxiety and withdrawal well beyond the reach of effective treat-ment.

* * *

Marietta could see what he was about to do. How he would pour the blood in the mouthlike sack on the side of the creature's head. Sacrificial blood, he had called it.

Hedley's eyes seemed now the size of small marbles. There was no expression in them whatsoever. Marietta sensed her daughter slipping, slipping away.

As she had been doing the past twenty minutes, Marietta encouraged the Indian to talk while she worked the ropes against the raw wood of the pillar. The ropes had begun to loosen.

The man turned to her now in the soft glow, away from the two young girls connected like tree branches to the creature in the center, and said, "She will want to kill you herself, bitch. For what you did to her daughter."

"The girl attacked me."

"Isn't that what white people always say?"

Just as he started to tilt the small bottle of blood into the sac on the side of the creature's head, the ropes worked loose enough to free Marietta's hands.

There was little time left. The man had explained that the creature could not function without sacrificial blood. It would not be able to fully take control of the girls without the sacrifice taking place. Marietta chose to believe that this meant her daughter was not yet beyond help—

She sprang from her feet, her hands out viselike to seize his throat. She slammed him into the wall, knocking the bottle of blood from his hands. She glimpsed it peripherally. He had left the cap on. Nothing seemed to have spilled.

He stabbed her once in the shoulder and once more in the area of her rib cage. She had been distracted by the bottle flying from her hands. He had produced the Bowie knife with calm expertise and cut her with almost clinical skill.

For the first time tonight, she felt herself becoming hysterical. The blood was flowing from her so fast . . .

5

BY THE TIME THEY REACHED THE CABIN, both Jody and David were out of breath and pasty with sweat that stung eyes, nostrils, and lips.

The smell reached Jody immediately. She turned her head away from the porch and cupped her hands over her nose. "God."

"I wonder what it is," David said.

Jody had dropped her hands. She straightened her back. "Let's go inside."

Neither of them had forgotten the scream that came from here a few minutes ago.

Jody went up on the porch. The whole cabin tilted and the aged wood groaned. The odor—like that of a wet dog —grew worse the closer she got to the screen door.

She opened the door and went inside. "David, come here."

Two steps behind, he drew up close enough to put his hand on her shoulder. Jody pointed to a large, twisted form on the floor. A gray-haired Indian woman. She had been stabbed.

David walked over to her, knelt, raised one plump arm to search for a pulse. He shook his head and placed her arm gently back on the floor.

By now Jody was looking around. The cabin was a junk heap of broken furniture, shabby clothes, and food-stuffs of various kinds that had been left to spoil in the ninety-degree heat. There was no light except for the shadowy illumination offered by a stray patch of moon-light.

She was just about to speak to David when they both heard the noise from beneath them. A wailing sound.

"How do you get down there?" Jody asked, frantic now.

"Must be some kind of trapdoor."

They fell to their feet and began crawling around the floor, looking for the seams of the door. Jody's left hand inadvertently slid into a puddle of warm, sticky blood. She knew better than to scream. But she did groan.

"Here," she said after a minute. She had found the metal ring that pulled the trapdoor up.

Her mind sensing that Jenny was below, she acted without caution, yanking the trapdoor back and peering into the watery green glow below.

The chill and the even worse odors of the basement got to her immediately. She clamped a hand over her mouth, afraid she was going to vomit.

The roaring began then. Her second husband had twice gone big game hunting, bringing back for his trouble not trophies but films of the safari. On one film he'd captured the sound of a bull elephant dying, a cry that seemed to shake the African sun itself. That's all she could think of now. That cry.

"No! Please!" she heard a man call out from below. Then came the sound of bones breaking, that peculiar snapping sound of a human being crushed. Then the man was silent.

"Jody," David said, pulling her back from the trap-door. They spoke in whispers.

"Jenny's down there!"

"It won't do any good for you to get killed. We should get some help. We don't know what's going on down there."

"It's too far for help." She nodded across the room. "I tried the phone. Somebody tore the cord from the wall."

They heard the sharp sound of the metal ladder being righted once more. Heavy footsteps began to clang their way upwards. In a few moments, whoever it was would show his or her face.

Jody and David crouched in the shadows behind a large cedar chest. Jody dug her nails deep into David's hand, deep enough to draw blood. David held her.

They both kept their eyes fixed on the open trapdoor.

The clanging of the heavy footsteps was now joined by a panting sound. All Jody could think of was somebody on a life support system.

The closer the clanging came, the closer the tortured breathing came, the more angry Jody became. Certainly this had to be the person who had taken her Jenny from her.

Her mind reeled at the sight of the hand that came out of the square opening of the trapdoor. It wasn't a hand at all. Not a human hand. It was black and leathery and had three clawlike digits with horned nails on each.

David held her tighter. In the slender patch of moon-light, he saw the clawlike hand, too.

But not even the hand could prepare them for what came next. Curiously, when she saw the head, Jody did not scream. Rather she drew in tighter to David and thought back through the years to her thirteenth summer, when she had been pursuing the man now at her side. That summer . . . and the strange grasshopperlike head she had seen silhouetted on a curtain.

The creature appeared.

This was the same creature, the body of a woman, albeit a very old woman, and the reptilian, helmeted head of a grasshopper.

"Sit tight," David said, seeing that the grasshopper was looking around the room and would in moments find them. "There's a crowbar over there," he whispered.

He was halfway to the crowbar when the creature saw him and turned with bulky precision in David's direction.

With a hand capable of almost invisible speed, the creature's clawed fingers reached David's throat and began squeezing. Jody could see the human muscles in the old woman's arms begin working tighter, tighter.

David dangled from the creature's grasp for nearly thirty seconds before Jody could reach the crowbar. With the metal rod, she slammed the grasshopper's head from the rear. There was a wailing—once again, elephantlike —but the creature did not drop David. Indeed, it put a second hand on his throat and began to squeeze.

Jody moved around to the front of the creature this time. Between David's head and the creature's shoulder was a space of perhaps half a foot. If she could only hit the creature on one of its bulbous eyes . . .

She had no warning that the creature was going to take its right arm away from David's throat and reach out and grab her.

The pain and loss of breath came instantly as the creature began choking her.

In vain she tried slamming the crowbar against the leathery head. She tried kicking, biting, scratching, but it became obvious quickly that the creature was far stronger than both of them together.

She saw David slip into unconsciousness. One moment he had been fighting with fists and feet, the next he was a lumpen mass of flesh. His legs and feet swung like pendulums as the creature first lifted then hurled him into the corner. He smashed through a wobbly kitchen table on the way down to the floor.

Now the creature had two hands to use on Jody.

In the basement, Jenny came to awareness with a blinding headache and a body covered with chilled sweat. She had no idea where she was. Her last memory was of sitting in her bedroom with her new Madonna album when the babysitter had asked her if she could come in and talk. Flattered by an older girl's attention, Jenny had of course said yes.

Then she remembered—

Here her mind paused. It did not *want* to recall what had happened next. The changing contours of the babysitter's face. The tube that emerged from the grasshopperlike face. Jenny's own screams and useless cries for help—

But where was she now?

She felt cold, damp walls. She felt hard-packed floors. She reached forward and felt a rounded piece of metal. She reached further up and felt an identical piece of metal.

She tilted her head way back and looked up at the square patch of shadowy light. There was an entrance way at the end of the ladder. She could climb up and—

It was then that she heard Grandma Jody. Most definitely Grandma Jody. Jenny knew she was not imagining this.

Pressing her hands down flat so that she could push herself up, she brushed against a body. In the darkness, she felt enough of the face and chest to know that the body was a human male. But she also knew, because the body was so still, that the man was dead.

She pulled her hand away. As she did so, her wrist banged against something sharp, cutting her instantly. A knife.

Grandma Jody shouted again, though Jenny could tell it was getting more and more difficult for Grandma Jody to even open her mouth.

Without thinking, Jenny grabbed the knife and ran over to the metal ladder.

As Jody was driven backwards by the creature, her hands moved about wildly, hoping to find something heavy she could pick up and use as a weapon. Once, her fingers touched the handle of an iron skillet. She felt an absurd optimism. She would pick it up and smash it down on the creature's head.

Just then the creature, apparently enraged that it had not yet killed Jody, slammed her into the wall, doubling the strength of its grip on her throat.

This time she felt it for sure. A peculiar chill, a cessation of sensory data that she knew to be death. It was mostly a cold, harsh odor in her lungs and nostrils. Sight went, then hearing, then even smell. The ceaseless pressure of the creature's hands on her throat and the vague knowledge that her head was being smacked, and smacked hard, against the wall.

At first, she did not recognize the significance of what

was taking place behind the creature. When she did understand it, she rejected it as illusion. It was impossible, her dying fantasy of rescue.

She watched as the fantasy, in the form of Jenny bearing the Indian man's knife, came up carefully behind the creature and plunged the knife deep into its spine.

Once again, Jody was able to hear. The creature's cry was, at the same time, repellent and pitiable.

Jenny yanked the bloody blade from the creature. As it turned its cumbersome grasshopper head toward her, Jenny plunged the knife into the side of its face.

The cry this time was even more chilling.

The creature, apparently given to panic, let Jody slide to the floor, and turned its attention to Jenny. Amber puslike fluid streamed from the facial wound.

Jenny, seeing that the creature was about to lunge at her, skillfully moved herself to the other side of the TV set. She dragged a chair over and pushed it into the set, trying to make the creature's passage as difficult as possible.

Jody, her senses gradually beginning to return, still watched all this as if it were a fantasy, or some improbable TV show. She tried to feel the reality of the moment. Jenny. Creature. Jenny in trouble.

Now Jenny was screaming—

The creature had moved through Jenny's fragile little fortress with no difficulty at all. Quickly, competently, its pincers lashed out and took Jenny's throat, just as they had taken Jody's.

It raised Jenny up and put her flat against the wall. It would not take long for a little girl like Jenny to die—

Jody forced herself to her feet, shaking her head, and shouted, "Stop! Stop!"

Her voice sounded faraway and unreal. Was that really her?

By instinct she found the handle of the iron skillet she had almost picked up when she was being strangled. She wasted no time. Skillet ready to use, she came up behind the creature and began smashing the skillet against its head.

Long after Jenny had sunk to the floor, unconscious but alive, Jody went on smashing the creature's head, thinking of all the young girls it had destroyed.

Sometime during her frenzy, David Fairbain came to consciousness, saw what was going on, and came over to take her hand from the skillet.

The first thing they did was splash water on Jenny's face and bring her to. The first thing Jenny did was to tell them about Hedley and Marietta Stover in the basement.

Epilogue

TWO WEEKS LATER, ON A MILD SUMMER
afternoon when the grass was a blue-green and the sky a
flawless blue, Jenny, Sam, David Fairbain, and Jody got
into David's big yellow Buick station wagon and drove to
the train depot. Earlier, they had stopped by the hospital
to see Marietta and Hedley, who were doing fine ("We're
going to be brave about it and have a good life, aren't we,
honey?" Marietta said as she stroked Hedley's hand).

Jenny insisted on sitting in the backseat with Grandma
Jody. She also insisted on holding her hand and kind of
snuggling with her every few minutes.

The route they took brought them past the old neighborhood where Jody had grown up. She saw the house
where she and her parents had lived, first her mom and
her real dad and then her mom and Uncle Bob. Sight of
the house almost shocked her. It was much smaller than

she'd recalled and, given its general state of disrepair, shabby to the eye. She felt cheated and foolish, as if memory had played a cruel joke on her, reminding her in the harshest terms that memory is the biggest illusion of all.

"Grandma Jody's crying," Jenny said.

Sam turned around. David looked at Jody in the rearview mirror.

"What's wrong, Mom?" Sam asked, obviously concerned.

"Oh, nothing." Jody laughed through her tears. "I just realized that I'm getting old. And starting to suffer old people's delusions."

David said, "It better not be a delusion that you're coming back here in two weeks, and that we're getting married."

She reached forward and patted his shoulder. "That part's not a delusion, David, I promise."

"Goody!" Jenny said, hugging Grandma.

Jody turned her eyes once more to the neighborhood. If she listened carefully, she could hear her own young voice calling out instructions in a sweet spring dusk for pom-pom pullaway or doing her Jerry Lewis impersonation. And if she watched just so, she could see herself on her Schwinn, and in her first pink party dress, or watching with fastidious attention the exploits of "The Range Rider."

Distantly, she could hear the summer circus and see herself on the midway, all cotton candy and kewpie dolls, yearning for this or that boy boldly standing up inside his ferris wheel box and dispensing papal-like smiles to all the girls below.

Had she ever really been young, or was that just an old person's delusion as she'd said to Sam?

Then they were out of the neighborhood, the Buick finding its bright confident way to the ancient red brick depot, Jody in the backseat feeling strangely isolated from those she loved.

She had quit crying now, but she knew the tears would come again. She wasn't even sure what the tears were about. She supposed they were about her memories of her frail Grandpa and busy bustling Mom and handsome Dad killed at war. She supposed they were about the way sunlight and shadow played on the surface of Cummings Creek and about the thrill of listening to "The Lone Ranger" on the radio in the darkness of her bedroom. She supposed they were about the way her three-month-old kitten had been hit by a Packard one day.

Yes, those were the reasons for her tears—those and so many other memories that she felt insane with their number and richness—because somewhere in the middle of those memories was a frightened, lonely girl named Jody.

A girl who had inexplicably become Grandma Jody. She reached out and touched Sam's hand. She was going to get better, Sam was. Jody was going to see to it. Jody was now going to become the mother she'd never quite been—it was never too late to bind up your child in your love. Never.

She reached over now and drew Jenny to her. She hugged her all the rest of the way to the depot while Sam looked at them and smiled.

THE ULTIMATE IN HORROR

FROM ST. MARTIN'S PRESS

HOW TO WIN AT
NINTENDO

Jeff Rovin

The ultimate home entertainment system, Nintendo is an unrivaled source of excitement and challenge. The key to winning is discovering the codes, strategies and maneuvers that are players' most closely guarded secrets. And *How to Win at Nintendo* can help you get to the top of your form! Now packed with more vital information than ever, the new updated and expanded edition of *How to Win at Nintendo* covers all of your favorite games!

Nintendo computer games are products of Nintendo of America Inc., which has neither authorized nor endorsed this book.

HOW TO WIN AT NINTENDO updated edition
_____ 92018-0 $3.95 U.S. _____ 92019-9 $4.95 Can.

And look for *How to Win at Nintendo* Volume II—coming in November '89!